THE QUEEN OF HEARTS

THE QUEEN OF HEARTS

TALES OF MIDDLE-AGE PASSION

BY MILLIE CRACE-BROWN

GREYCORE
New York

COVER ART: Valerie van Inwegen (V Scott V)
COVER AND TEXT DESIGN: Kathleen Massaro

Crace-Brown, Millie
    The Queen of Hearts: tales of middle-age passion / by Millie
Crace-Brown
    p. cm
    LCCN: 99-90608
    ISBN: 0-9671851-7-3

    1. Middle-aged women—Fiction. 2. Divorced mother—Fiction
3. Substance abuse—Fiction
I. Title.

PS3553R195QQ44 2000   813'.54
            QB199-598

For Polly

THE QUEEN
OF HEARTS

ROSIE WAS ON HER HANDS AND KNEES, scrubbing scum out from between the tiles in the bathroom with a toothbrush. The stereo was on in the other room, and she was keeping time to Dion's *King of the New York Streets*. The volume was up, and as she was singing along with the tune, she didn't hear her son pull up outside. Ordinarily she would have heard him long before he reached the driveway (his car had only half a muffler), and, because he always came in with three or four other eighteen-year-olds, either locked the bathroom door or dashed up to her room to make herself presentable. As it was, she happened to look over her shoulder and there they were, four thin giants in baggy T-shirts, ill-fitting scruffed-up leather jackets, and combat boots, framed together in the doorway so that they looked like an animated version of one of Jason's death metal posters. Jason was saying something about where they were off to next while the others took turns competing with Dion to chant, "Hi, Mrs. Campbell."

Rosie returned Jason's friends' greetings and nodded an acknowledgment to whatever Jason had said. Then the boys vanished from the hallway as suddenly as they had appeared and Rosie used her foot to close the bathroom door. The stereo went off, and Dion was instantly replaced by the sound of youthful laughter, the refrigerator door banging closed, cabinets flying open, and the tinkle of glasses and dishes being set out. Rosie, who had stopped scrubbing, wondered whether it was her singing voice or the sight of her big ass, which had been facing right up at them, that had triggered their mirth. With the toothbrush still in her hand, she swept her arm back and felt for holes in the baggy sweat pants that she always wore to clean. Finding none, she bent her head and looked into the neckline of her T-shirt to examine, beyond her small encased breasts, the fleshy protuberance of her stomach. It could have been worse, she said to herself; she could have been facing the door. "Good-bye, Mrs. Campbell," Jason's friends called from the kitchen. The door slammed. Car doors opened and shut in the driveway. Then the motor roared to life and screeched into reverse.

Rosie flung an arm over the top of the vanity and hauled herself into a standing position. It wasn't until her face appeared in the mirror that she remembered that she had used a rubber band to pull her hair together at the top of her head so that it wouldn't get in her way while she worked. She was ridiculous, she decided, a fat, middle-aged woman with her hair sticking straight up, scrubbing scum to the blast of rock and roll in clothes the Salvation Army wouldn't have taken. Of course the Salvation Army wouldn't have taken the clothes that Jason and his friends wore either, but that was different; there was a name for their disarray, 'grunge' Rosie thought it was, and it marked them as being a part of a brotherhood that shunned Rosie's type.

She waddled into the kitchen to inspect the damage. There were glasses out on the counter, two of them still half full of milk. The plates and forks had made it to the sink, but a trail of crumbs revealed the path they had taken. She opened the refrigerator and removed the glass pie plate. She had made the pie yesterday, and she and Frank, who both had cholesterol problems, had shared a small piece last night. Now there was nothing left but the parts of the crust that had clung to the edge of the plate. She popped them loose with her fingers and ate them quickly, so that she wouldn't have time to consider the consequences. The boys too, she knew, had eaten standing up. They always did; they were always in a hurry. They gulped their drinks and swallowed their snacks without chewing, talking all the while about other people, the things that happened at school, laughing so hard that sometimes one or the other felt compelled to let his food drop out of his mouth, and then laughing harder yet.

Rosie loved her son. He sulked in the house, because it was boring and there was nothing to do, but she knew that in his other life, his life with his friends, he was good-natured, agreeable, and well-liked. And he was funny too, to Rosie's way of thinking. For example, if he was home when she pulled into the driveway, he often flew out of the house, and pretending that he had some all important message to relate to her, ran into her car just as she was stopping, bounced off it, and then lay on the ground feigning paroxysm. Frank, who was worried about the loans they would be taking out in September for Jason's college education, grumbled when he exhibited such behavior. Jason's grades were good, but Frank wished they were better. He was afraid that once Jason was away at school in another state, without any supervision whatsoever, his grades would bottom out and he'd wind up at some minimum wage job from which, for years to come, there would be no escape.

Although she didn't share Frank's fears, Rosie understood them; he was only projecting his own past failings onto the boy. Frank had started college in the late sixties, but as he had preferred partying to studying, his parents had withdrawn their support. He had worked at dozens of minimum wage jobs in that first half decade of his adult life. Then, when he was twenty-five, he met Rosie, fell in love with Rosie, and he got his second chance. Rosie, who was working for a publisher at that time, insisted he move from his room in the boarding house in Englewood Cliffs, New Jersey into her Manhattan apartment. She paid for rent and groceries and he paid for his part-time education with the money he made now from part-time jobs. Since she could edit books at home, she continued to earn a salary even after Jason was born, and by the time Jason was eight, Frank was a junior partner in a real estate law firm and making enough money for Rosie to quit her job if she wanted to. She hadn't wanted to, but Frank had found a house in Wycoff, New Jersey, a handyman special, and since Rosie was handy, Frank thought her time would be better spent there than with her manuscripts.

It had taken years to put the place in shape. When Jason left for college, it would be too big for them. They hadn't talked about that yet, but Rosie planned to bring up the subject in the near future. They had virtually no savings; a lot came in, but more went out. If they sold the house, which was now worth considerably more than what they had paid for it, they could buy a smaller place for cash and use what was left to take a trip. More than anything, Rosie wanted to spend a year in Europe. They had always planned to go when Frank retired, but Rosie didn't want to wait that long. Sometimes she got sharp pains on the right side of her head. Sometimes her heart palpitated.

Rosie was about to return to her work in the bathroom when she heard another car pulling into the driveway and ran instead to the window. To her surprise, it was Frank, home three hours earlier than usual. She pulled the rubber band out of her hair, and opening the door, yelled, "Honey! What's wrong?"

Frank, who was just getting out, looked up at her. "Nothing," he said.

She held the screen door open and as he passed her, she reached out and touched his forehead. "Are you sick? Do you feel well? Did something happen?"

He stepped into the kitchen and opened the refrigerator. "Where's the pie?" he asked.

Rosie smiled. "Jason—" she began.

Frank saw the dish in the sink and made a face. "The whole thing?"

"—and his friends."

Frank sighed and headed into the living room, toward the stairs. Following on his heels, Rosie cried, "Can I fix you something else? Do you want a sandwich? I have fruit. Do you want a piece of fruit? A kiwi maybe?"

They went up the stairs and into the bedroom, and Frank, who hadn't answered, plopped down on the bed and sighed deeply. "Rosie, Rosie, Rosie, Rosie," he said, shaking his head.

Rosie sank down beside him and ran her fingertips up and down the ridge of bone in the middle of his back. "I knew something was wrong. Tell me, Honey. Did something happen at work?"

Frank hung his head. "Yes," he breathed. "Something happened at work." He looked up, then down, then he sighed again.

"What?" Rosie shrieked. "Would you just tell me already! What happened?"

Frank cracked his knuckles and lowered his head even further, until it was only inches above his knees. "Sheila," he mumbled. "Sheila happened."

It took some doing, between the tears and running back and forth to the adjoining bathroom to blow her nose, but finally she managed to get it out of him. He was moving in with Sheila, his twenty-eight-year-old secretary. He felt relaxed with her, he professed. Rosie had met Sheila at an office party, a blue-eyed blonde with a chipped front tooth and a habit of rolling her shoulders back so that her blouse pulled against her breasts. She couldn't imagine Frank relaxing with her. But she was too preoccupied with getting him to pinpoint when this had all begun to remember to voice that opinion. For some reason, Frank couldn't recall when it had started. He had had lunch with her a few times, both out and at her apartment, but nothing, he swore, had happened. They had been friends. His feelings toward her had been, if anything, paternal. And then something changed, he didn't know when. If it had been clear, he insisted, he would have told Rosie. "These things just sneak up on you," he explained, his face so distorted with petition that it seemed about to liquefy.

"When?" Rosie croaked. "When are you leaving?"

"Now?" he asked, his brows lifting.

She stared at him in disbelief for nearly a minute. Then she lost it.

Jumping up from the bed, she tore his drawers out of his bureau and dropped them onto the floor. She swept her arm over the bureau top and sent the lamp and his loose change and credit card receipts flying. ("It's not my fault," she seemed to hear him saying. "It's not like I planned this.") She opened the closet doors and dislodged several of his shirts (which she had starched and ironed) from their hangers and threw them down on the floor and ran on them as if they were a tread mill. She picked up his shoes, and without any regard for his bowling trophies and other keepsakes, she hurled them one by one in the direction of the shelf across the room. She went into the bathroom and gathered his various medications from the cabinet above the sink and dropped them into the toilet bowl. ("Hey! Hey! Hey!" he shouted behind her.) She grabbed his shaving cream, pushed off the cap, and came at him. But the thing was practically empty and what little she could coax out dripped down the side of the can and onto her arm.

She threw the can at him. She removed the picture of his mother from the wall and, holding it like a Frisbee, whipped it into the wall opposite. Then she kicked at him, but he managed to jump away before she could do much damage. She called him every bad name she could think of, her words coming so fast that spittle flew from the sides of her mouth. But no matter how violently she behaved, she could not rid herself of the gnawing within, and eventually she gave up and went downstairs to lie on her back on the sofa.

When she had regulated her breathing, she noted that the stereo light was on; Jason had only lowered the stereo, not turned it off. A devotee of orderliness, she felt an urge to get up and attend to it, but in the end she wasn't able to respond. She was depleted now, entirely devoid of strength. She could hear Frank moving about upstairs, slowly, quietly packing his things. He'll come back, she thought to herself, and then she laughed bitterly; he wasn't even gone yet and already she was in denial.

When she heard him coming down the stairs, she closed her eyes and pretended to be asleep. His footsteps stopped near her, and she imagined that he was looking down on her, some small part of him grieving for all the time that they had put in together. Anticipating that he would say something reassuring, her name at the very least, she held her breath, but the next sound she heard was that of the door opening. She was on her feet immediately, pulling at the door as he was trying to shut it. "And what about Jason?" she screamed. "When does he get to hear the good news?"

Frank kept moving, down the steps and toward the car. When he reached it, he opened the trunk and put the solitary suitcase into it. In spite of her rage over this new issue, Rosie found herself thinking, He'll have to come back soon for more clothes. Thank God. He'll have to come back. "Who the hell is going to tell Jason?" she shouted.

He didn't even look at her. He simply got into the car and backed out of the driveway—not hurriedly, as Jason had, but slowly, deliberately, looking both ways when he reached the road—as if he were a man of caution.

"A party at my cousin's apartment in 1973," Rosie grumbled. She hated Blanche's office. It was entirely too small, and because Blanche kept the shades drawn, too dim for her to glean Blanche's reactions to her words. "Why do you want to know anyway? What good will dredging up all that do?"

"Every time you've been here," Blanche said softly, "we've talked about the end, what he said to you, how unexpected it all was, how just the night before you had been watching a movie together, sharing a piece of chocolate cream pie. Humor me just this once."

Another thing that Rosie hated was the restraint in Blanche's tone, a pretense, she felt certain, meant to make her patients feel out of control by comparison. She was tempted to point out that the older woman's wastepaper basket was full to the brim with Milky Way wrappers. "Okay, okay," she said, and she took a deep breath.

"He was sitting with a group of girls, pretty girls, vivacious types, just the opposite of me. They were passing a joint, laughing their heads off, choking on the pot. I thought he was incredibly handsome."

"But you didn't speak to him."

Rosie, who was pacing, made a sharp turn and clenched her fists. "No. I was too shy. And since he seemed to enjoy the company of the girls he was with, I had no reason to think he'd be interested in me. I watched him from a distance."

"And so how did you meet?"

Rosie stopped pacing and faced her. It occurred to her that she had never seen Blanche standing up; she had no idea how tall she was. "Do you mind if I smoke?" she asked.

Blanche lifted a finger to indicate the no smoking sign on the wall.

"Please," Rosie whined, her face as puffy as rising bread.

Expressionlessly, Blanche leaned over, put the shade up a few inches, and cracked the window. "Just one," she said sternly.

Rosie sat down on the sofa and fumbled in her bag. She had taken up smoking only recently, and as her hands were quaking, it took her

15

some moments to get the pack open and extract a cigarette. "My cousin, Max, who went to high school with Frank, had parties all the time," she said, exhaling smoke and shaking out the match vigorously. "And although we didn't get on very well, I called him, Max, regularly and pestered him until I got myself invited. I fantasized about Frank. I thought about him all the time, though after seven or eight parties over a course of as many months, it became clear that I would never get his attention. And then one day I went to my dentist's office, and there he was, sitting in the waiting room, flipping through a magazine. I couldn't believe it! I froze! Of course he looked up at me. Everyone did. I was just standing there with my mouth opened, blushing, blinking, unable to move, the door still opened behind me. Finally, one of the other patients, this little old lady, asked me to close the door. When I glanced at her, I came back into myself and got moving again. I took a seat in the far corner and opened the paperback I'd brought along and didn't look up from it until the receptionist appeared and called him in."

Rosie tapped her cigarette and caught the ashes in the palm of her other hand. Sighing almost imperceptibly, Blanche opened a desk drawer and extracted an ashtray. "A month or so later," Rosie continued, "Max had another party, and Frank recognized me." She coughed out a bitter laugh, and with it a cloud of smoke. "He came up to me and asked me how my teeth were doing. My friend Grace, who I'd come with and who knew that I was crazy about him, proceeded to tell him all about me—my job, my apartment—while I stared down at Frank's scruffy high tops. When she finished her soliloquy, which embarrassed me terribly, Grace mumbled a farewell and stepped aside. I looked up at Frank. He was smiling...you know, bemusedly. Beyond him I could see the group of girls that he usually spent the evening with, one of whom was watching us. I was certain that if I didn't say something clever within the next few seconds, he'd turn around and head back to them. And the next thing I knew my mouth opened and I was saying, 'I'd like to have dinner with you sometime.' Can you imagine! It just came out of my mouth without any warning whatsoever! I was horrified. I could have died right there on the spot! I'd never done anything like that in my life! The blood was pounding so hard in my ears that it took a moment for me to realize that he'd accepted my invitation and was waiting for me to give him my number."

Rosie stubbed out the cigarette, which she had smoked down to the butt, and got up to pace again. "I was sure it wouldn't last. I was tight, nervous, painfully shy; I seldom spoke above a whisper. And of course I wasn't like I am now, but even then I was dumpy, you know, thick around the waist and thighs." She hesitated for a moment, concerned that she might have insulted Blanche, who, at least from the waist up, was fairly corpulent herself. "And he was so handsome," she went on. "And so easy going. He laughed all the time, said whatever he was thinking. Whenever we parted, I expected not to hear from him again, but a week or so would pass and I would. Finally I got my nerve up and asked him what he saw in me, and he explained that he was looking to change his life, that he had to get serious before it was too late, that he needed my influence. It's kind of funny, you know? The reason I was attracted to him was because I was looking to become more frivolous. I mean, it was the early seventies! People were loose. And here I had this fancy uptown job and all these business clothes in the closet…

"It lasted; what can I say? We both got what we wanted. He could concentrate, he said, in my quiet apartment where the telephone seldom rang. So I suggested he move in. He wanted to give college another try. I helped him write his application essays. I guided him toward the best books, the best classical music, the kinds of clothes to wear on job interviews. And he taught me how to smoke pot, how to choose the best rock and roll albums, how to dance to rock and roll. He bought me long flowing skirts and diaphanous blouses, things I had always admired but never would have had the nerve to wear without him by my side. On week nights he studied and I read. On weekends, we went to parties or had our own. I felt positively foolhardy!

"Of course we had to give up the partying when Frank got into law; Frank insisted. Or rather, we had parties, but now they were entirely different. Dinner for six, you know…candles on the table, soft music, stimulating conversation instead of shrieks of wild laughter." She looked up abruptly. "It never occurred to me, Blanche, that I would have to face old age alone. I mean, I've seen this happen to other women over the years, but I never thought it would happen to me."

"Well, now you'll have to come up with an alternative plan," Blanche said softly.

"An alternative plan!" Rosie screeched. "I related my alternative plan last week! You can't have forgotten! I want to die! My plan is to kill myself."

As if to let Rosie hear for herself how ridiculous she sounded, Blanche let a moment pass before speaking. "If that were true, you'd have done it already. It's been a month. You've gotten through the worst of it, don't you think?"

"I'm waiting until Jason is gone," Rosie grumbled. "Then I'm going to do it."

Blanche, who had been sitting back in her recliner, sat forward. "Our time is just about up for today, Rosie, but before you leave, I'm going to give you a prescription."

"That's what I want," Rosie cried, and she planted her fists on Blanche's desk. "That's how I plan to do it."

Rosie spent her days and nights reclining on the sofa, dressed in a T-shirt and her cleaning pants, sometimes staring at the TV and sometimes at the ceiling. It didn't matter which; whatever she looked at, the only thing she saw was Frank, as he had been that day up in their bedroom when he had come home early to announce his plans. He called her once, to see how she was doing and to let her know that he intended to put the house up for sale and was forwarding paperwork for her to sign, and they chatted nicely for the first few minutes. But then Rosie broke down and began pleading with him to come home, and eventually Frank hung up on her. She didn't turn on lights anymore after that. From the moment she awakened in the morning, she looked forward solely to dusk, when she would lose herself, occasionally, in the gradual disintegration of her surroundings.

Jason didn't seem to have an opinion one way or the other about his father's departure. And except for the fact that he now left his friends waiting in the car when he had to come in for something, he gave no indication that he was aware of Rosie's state. "Hi, Mom," he called on the way in, "Bye, Mom," on the way out again, and "Night, Mom," when he came home for good. He was invited to Sheila's once for dinner, but for all that Rosie spent a good deal of emotional energy interrogating him, he could not be made to say more than, "She's okay."

Eventually Rosie stopped trying to talk to him; she merely mumbled back the same number of syllables that he mumbled to her. Nor did she answer the phone anymore when it rang. The few close friends she had, who had been supportive initially, when Rosie was still raging, were only tiresome now. They seemed to think that she should be getting back on her feet, going to support groups, starting a new life—as if that were a possibility. Rosie was like a machine that had gone on the blink. Until Frank left, she had been a creature of routine, a disciple of the habitual. She had paid bills on Mondays, shopped on Tuesdays, volunteered at the library on Wednesdays, written up and typed Frank's office newsletter on Thursdays, and cleaned on Fridays. And as she had carried out all of these various assignments between the hours of ten and four, the hours before and after were likewise allocated for specific purposes. She had taken her morning walks at eight, breakfasted and read the paper at nine, begun cooking dinner at four, served it at six, tidied up at seven, watched TV with Frank from eight till ten, and then read her novels until exactly 11:30, when she would go to bed.

Now she did none of the above. There was no reason to pay the bills; by the time the collection agencies got around to looking her up, she'd be gone. As for the shopping, she had given Jason a check for $1000 and he now ate all his meals out, at Pizza Hut or at McDonald's. And there was easily enough canned food in the walk-in pantry to last Rosie until September. The librarian, who was a friend of Rosie's, had suggested she take some time, and of course Frank would not expect his newsletter anymore. And each time she considered cleaning the house, she was defeated immediately by the recollection of her bedroom, which she had never put back to order after the day she demolished it. The rest of the house didn't get dirty.

Jason only came home to sleep, and Rosie only left the sofa to use the bathroom or to heat up a can of soup. She stopped smoking when she ran out of cigarettes. And she had not been to see Blanche since she got the prescription.

Blanche had told Rosie that it would take approximately three weeks for the Zakcor to take effect, but four had passed and Rosie felt no different. She couldn't have cared less; she had everything she needed—pillow, quilt, remote control, and a roof over her head—to wait it out until September. Then, as soon as Jason left for college, she planned to start swallowing, whatever was left of the Zakcor first and afterwards whatever else she could find in the house. She had envisioned the process a thousand times; she would start with the medicine cabinet in the downstairs bathroom, then proceed to the cabinet beneath the sink. And if she was still ambulatory after all that, she'd head for the basement, where she kept her paint cans, weed killers, and the gasoline that she used for the lawnmower.

One night Rosie felt a spark of animation and sat up. She had been thinking about something that had happened years ago, and she found she had a mild but authentic urge to call someone and tell them about it. But when she glanced at the VCR clock across the room, she saw that it was nearly midnight, far too late to be making calls to anyone she knew. She was just about to lie down again and await the resumption of her lethargy when Jason's muffler proclaimed his impending arrival.

"Jason," she called when he entered.

Jason gasped. "You scared me, Ma," he said.

"Sit down. I want to talk to you."

Jason sat in the rocker across the room and turned on the lamp, but when he saw Rosie's features compress in reaction to the rush of light, he quickly turned it off again.

"Jason," she began, "I want to tell you about something that happened when you were born."

"I'm tired, Mom. I got school—"

"Your father and I had a dog at the time, a medium-sized black thing, a mutt. A couple we knew was moving and had to get rid of him, and we volunteered to take him. Petey, his name was. But he was old when we got him, and by the time I was due to deliver you, he had slowed down to the point where he could barely lift his head to his bowl to eat. And he was testy too. We decided that the humane thing to do would be to put him to sleep."

"Ma—"

"Listen! We took him to the vet, after hours, about six, and watched as he gave him the injection. It was very sad. I mean, we weren't attached to Petey the way his original owners had been, but all the same we had had some pretty good times together, and your father and I felt miserable about the whole thing. And just after the injection, just before he passed, Petey looked up at me with those big brown eyes, as if to say—"

"Mom, please—"

"—and then, after, after he…was dead, after the vet and your father and I had spent some moments talking about Petey and then about dogs generally, the vet, Dr. Saddler, informs us that we have to bury Petey ourselves, that he isn't prepared to dispose of him for us!

"Well! We were still living in the city then of course, in the apartment. There was that little courtyard, but that was for everyone's use; we couldn't very well bury Petey back there. Then your father got the bright idea that we should drive over the bridge, into New Jersey, and bury him in your grandfather's back yard. So, with Dr. Saddler's help, we wrapped Petey in a piece of plastic and put him into the back seat—because it seemed sort of callous to put a thing that had only just been alive, though barely, in the trunk. And we're driving along, very solemn, recalling all the cute things that Petey had done when we had first inherited him and he was still somewhat mobile, and we cross the bridge, and we're on Route 4, and all of a sudden your father pulls into a restaurant parking lot and parks! I said, 'Frank, what are you doing?' And he said, 'I'm hungry. It's late. We'll get something to eat.' And I said, 'No way am I going into a restaurant with a dead dog in the back of the car. We'll bury him, and then we'll think about our stomachs.'"

"Mom, why are you—"

"Well, we had quite an argument after that. It was summer and the car windows were down and I'm sure we amused a good many passersby with me yelling, 'But Frank, he's dead!' and your father yelling back, 'That's the point! So why not eat? ' You see, your father's thinking was that it was still a twenty minute ride to your grandfather's, and then we'd have to go in and explain what we we're doing there, and then go in the garage and find the shovel and dig the grave…His point was that it would be hours until we were done, that by the time we got to stop for dinner, all the restaurants would be closing up. I suppose that was logical, but I simply couldn't imagine going in to eat, at a fancy place no less, with a dead dog in the back seat of the car. So, to make a long story short, your father went in without me."

"Mom, I don't care—"

"I was fuming, Jason. You can't imagine. I kept turning around and looking at Petey. Except for the plastic, he didn't look any different than he had before the injection. And it bothered me, the plastic.

I felt an urge to go back there and rip it off him. I felt as if it were me rolled up in it, as if I was suffocating. And I believe I would have gone back and removed it, except at some point I realized that Petey was beginning to stink—"

"Ma!"

"—which only made me more angry. I must have been out there an hour. Your father, who was just as angry as I was, was taking his good old time. And I had just decided to call a cab and get home on my own when I got my first contraction."

"Mom, I know the rest—"

"No you don't!" Rosie shouted. "You only know the details concerning your birth, how long you were and how much you weighed. Your father would never let me repeat this part of it because it upset him too much, and so I never did. Now you listen to me, young man. You stay put and hear what happened, you hear?"

"Okay, okay. Would you calm down already?"

Rosie took several deep breaths. "Okay, so where was I?"

"You got your first—"

"Right. Thank you. I got my first contraction. And having never had a baby before, I was scared to death. I ran into the restaurant, and there's your father, eating a piece of chocolate forest cake all by himself at a table meant for four. I didn't have to say a word. The look on my face and the position of my hands on my stomach told him everything. He pulled a twenty from his pocket and threw it on the table and off we went, back into the car, back over the bridge, into the traffic, dodging cars, running lights…"

"Ma, can you get to the point?"

"I'm getting there, Jason!"

"Okay, okay."

"Okay. Well, we got there, finally. And the doctor came in. And he had your father put on this green surgical outfit, same as he was wearing, and—"

Rosie broke off laughing. "Would you hurry it up, Ma?" Jason cried over her.

It took her several minutes to answer, because she could only cram one or two words in between each burst of laughter. "The point...is that...I was...in labor with you for...twenty-eight hours!"

"Yeah, so?"

"And...your father...stayed with me...the entire time!"

"Yeah, so what?"

"So what!...Petey...."

But Rosie was crying now, laughing and crying simultaneously, whooping and wailing so fiercely that she couldn't go on. Nor did she hear Jason holler, "Night, Mom," as he bolted up the stairs in the dark.

Rosie went through her albums first thing in the morning. Then, having found what she wanted, she set the needle in place, and taking the stairs two at a time, rushed up the stairs and burst into Jason's room. Jason opened his eyes just in time to see her standing in his doorway with her legs apart and her spread arms out, just in time to hear her shout, along with James Brown, "I FEEEEEL GOOD!"

"What the hell...?" Jason mumbled.

But Rosie, who was dancing around the room now, snapping her fingers, leaping over the piles of clothes on the floor, didn't hear him. "So good," she sang bending forward, "so good," bending back, "since I got you," and she wiggled down until she was crouching and at eye level with Jason, whose mouth was wide open and whose eyes were as round as marbles. "Get up and dance with your mother," she coaxed.

"You're gone, Mom!" he cried.

"Oh, I should have known you'd be unkind," she said, and she jumped up and began to dance again.

But Jason sat up and shouted, "No, Mom, I mean you're gone!" so loud and with such emphasis that Rosie turned back toward him and looked where he was looking, at her body. She bent forward and pulled her sweat pants tight around her thighs. Then she straightened and put her hands on her waist. "Oh, my God," she muttered.

Rosie ran out of the room, through her own room and into the bathroom, and carefully avoiding the sight of Frank's medications, which were all still floating in the toilet, she jumped on the scale. When the numbers finally stopped convulsing, she saw, to her astonishment, that she had lost forty-six pounds.

After Jason left for school, Rosie found an old butterfly net in the basement and used it to fish Frank's little bottles out of the toilet. Then, giggling maniacally, she used tongs to place the medications in a shoe box, which she wrapped and addressed to Frank at his office. Afterwards, she drew the shades on all the windows, changed into a bathing suit that she had worn many years earlier, and cleaned the house from top to bottom. When everything was glittering again, she took an extremely long shower, her first in weeks. It was Tuesday; she made an appointment to have her hair cut on Wednesday, to shop with her friend Lois on Thursday, and to see Blanche on Friday. Then she had herself a can of tuna for dinner and went to bed with *The New Columbia Encyclopedia*, which she had always meant to read but had never got around to starting. She was up to an entry on aerial photography when she finally began to tire, and thus it is no surprise that she found herself flying in her dreams.

Before her transformation, Rosie had worn her dark hair straight and just long enough to conceal her double chin from the side. At a hundred and eighty-five pounds, she had long since given up finding jeans and blouses to fit and had settled instead for muumuus for social events and men's sweat suits, which always fit better than women's, for leisure time. As far as adornments went, Rosie had abandoned them back after Jason was born, when the weight came— or rather, when it became clear that it would not go away. She had worn no make-up, no jewelry, no perfume, nothing at all which might call attention to a body she had wished only to conceal. So when the receptionist admitted her into Blanche's shadowy office on Friday, it was no wonder that Blanche lifted a finger and mumbled, "I'm Doctor Williams. Doctor Watts is down the hall."

"No, it's me," Rosie cried, delighted, and she spun around so that Blanche could get a good look.

Blanche gasped audibly, leaned over to put up the window shade, and gasped again.

"The haircut cost me $65," Rosie said. "Can you imagine that?" She patted the rigid spikes on the top of her head. "I just went in and told this child—she couldn't have been much older than Jason—to do whatever she wanted to me. At first I didn't like it, but on the way home I stopped at a jewelry store and got all these wild earrings." She tilted her head and pushed one lobe forward in case Blanche might have missed the colorful beaded ornament that nearly grazed her shoulder. Then she ran her hand down her chest. "The dress was actually a few dollars cheaper than the haircut. First I had on one the same color but more in the style of what I used to wear. But then one of the attendants came over with this one and said, 'Honey, why would you want to hide a waistline like yours with a shift?' So I wound up with this. Do you like it?"

"My God," Blanche said without moving her lips.

"As for the make-up, it's this new subtle-look stuff." She laughed abruptly. "Well, I guess it's not new, but it was to me." She leaned over Blanche's desk and turned her head from side to side. "See? It looks like I don't have any on. And the bra is padded, in case you're wondering, though only slightly. I figured I might as well do everything. Of course none of it will last. I couldn't eat, you see. But now my appetite's improving already. I'll look like my old self again in no time. But in the meantime, I thought, Why not have a little fun, right? Anyway, Frank paid for everything."

"You mean—"

"Yes, American Express. I sent Frank a note and explained about the charges and offered to reimburse him once the house is sold. I figured he wouldn't mind. He must be charging up a storm himself because he hasn't been back for the rest of his clothes. Did I tell you that he put the house on the market? "

"Well," Blanche managed.

"Oh, and I almost forgot. I have a job interview. Can you imagine? After all these years?"

Blanche cleared her throat. "Then I suppose we should start there. How do you feel about—"

"I feel great! But I don't have time to discuss it now. I only came by to show you—"

"But you've been out of the work force for years," Blanche cried.

"You must have some reservations. I think we should talk—"

Rosie reached for the door. "I'd love to, but I'll be late if I don't leave this instant."

Rosie knew next to nothing about herbs when she was hired to work at the herbary, but the proprietor, a young woman named Gail whose hair was as pale and as kinky as cotton candy, was unconcerned. Gail spent most of her day discussing the fine details of her customers' ailments with them and choosing just the right combination of herbs to alleviate them; all she really needed was someone to tend to the cash register and to keep the shelves clean and well-stocked. Rosie, however, listened intently as she worked, and in no time at all she had acquired enough knowledge to be able to advise those with mild afflictions while Gail concentrated on the more serious cases.

A man came in one day while Gail was out to lunch. Between his bushy gray hair and brows and beard, all Rosie could see of his face were his ruddy cheeks and his eyes, which were blue and punctuated by deep laugh lines. The sawdust on the edge of his flannel shirt pocket indicated that he worked in construction. When Rosie asked if she could help him, he looked over one shoulder and then the other. And although it was clear that he was the only customer in the small shop, he stepped up close and whispered, "Indigestion."

You could always tell the ones who were venturing into the herbary for the first time. They behaved as if they were consorting with witches and would sooner die than have anyone know. When the door opened behind him, the poor fellow stiffened. Then, holding Rosie's gaze for all he was worth, he nodded almost imperceptibly. And Rosie, understanding that he didn't want to discuss his ailment any further, called to her new customer, "Have a look around, be with you in a minute," and turned to the shelf behind her to take down a box of chamomile tea and a bottle of dandelion extract. She placed them on the counter, and, once the hairy fellow had nodded an assent, she rang them up and put them into a paper bag. He nodded once more and left with his head down.

A week later he was back, and smiling. "It worked!" he called from the door.

"Good," Rosie said.

He stepped in and closed the door behind him. "No, I mean it really worked. I've had this problem for years. You have no idea! I've tried prescription drugs, but they didn't agree with me. You're incredible. How did you know?"

"I can't take any credit—" Rosie began, and she turned to look at Gail, who was smiling over the order that she was writing up at her desk in the corner behind the counter. "Of course you can," the man interrupted. "You cured me! You're a miracle-worker. Let me take you to lunch."

Throughout their lunch, grilled-cheese sandwiches at the diner across the street, Rosie tried to explain that her knowledge of herbs was only rudimentary, that Gail was the real miracle-worker, but that only got Les (his full name was Lester Charles Bakerson) going about how refreshingly modest she was. Then, while they were having coffee, he told her that he found her attractive, and when she tried to explain that she was actually fat and had a double chin, he said that her sense of humor was refreshing too. She gave up after that and asked him questions about himself. He was a cabinet-maker, it turned out. He'd been divorced for several years and had two grown children and a six-month-old grandson. He showed her pictures of his children and their spouses and the baby. She showed him Jason's picture.

On Friday night, Rosie found herself in Les's log cabin in Suffern, New York, where he was making her dinner. Since he wouldn't let her help, she sat in the living room looking at the various animal heads that protruded from the dark-paneled walls. There was a gun cabinet in one corner, which, he had told her earlier, he had built himself, and in it rifles and shotguns. Leaning against it was a fishing pole, and beside that, three metal tackle boxes.

Les stuck his head in from the other room. "You doing okay in there?" he asked.

Rosie saluted him with her wine glass. "Just fine."

Les, who was wearing a red apron and holding a wooden spoon in his hand, jutted his chin toward the moose above the fireplace. "That's George," he said.

"How do you do, George," Rosie said, and she smiled at Les, but he didn't smile back.

"It doesn't bother you?" Les asked.

Rosie looked about herself. "What?"

"George, the others, the guns. Some women don't like that sort of thing."

Rosie grinned. She was thinking of poor Petey that night eighteen years ago, deteriorating in a piece of plastic. When Frank had gotten into the car, so tired after the long labor that he could think of nothing but getting home and going to sleep, he had been overwhelmed immediately by the foul smell. He had jumped right back out and vomited several times in the hospital parking lot. At least Les's animals didn't stink. They looked friendly, in fact. "No," she answered.

"Okay, then, because I had to know." He stepped out of her view and then, seconds later, back into it again. "Because there was this woman last year," he continued.

"I took her out three, four, five times. And then I brought her here one night and she saw the guns and the rest of it and flipped out and insisted I take her home. She made me feel like an ax-murderer or something. I mean, I've never shot anything out of season and I never shoot more than my license says I can." He stopped to take a deep breath. "So I guess that's why I brought you here tonight. I wanted you to see who I am and how I live right from the get-go. Then, if you find it bothers you, well, we can call things off before they get started. I'm a hunter. I wanted you to know that."

Rosie nodded. Les nodded back at her. She bit her lip and looked down at her lap, at the *Gander Mountain* catalogue that she had spread across her knees, which, evidently, was where Les ordered all his clothing. "There's stuff you should know about me too," she said softly, but when she looked up, she saw that he had gone back into the kitchen.

Frank called Rosie the following morning, just as she was getting ready to leave for the herbary, to say that the real estate agent had contacted him and would be bringing over a potential buyer. "Is the house in order?" he asked.

The implication that it might not be assured her that he had not spoken to Jason in some time. "Yes," she said brightly. "Did you get your package in the mail?"

Frank cleared his throat. "Rosie, I realize that that little prank was merely a reaction to the sorrow I caused you, but—"

"No it wasn't, Frank, but let's not talk about that. Tell me, how's Sheila doing?"

"Well, actually, we're moving into a larger apartment. That's why it's very important that the house—"

"Oh, for crying out loud, Frank. Forget about the house. It looks fine. I'm sure it will sell in no time. Did Jason tell you that I got my hair cut?"

"Oh. How nice."

"Yes, and I had a date last night."

There was a long silence. Then Frank asked, "With a man?"

"Yes, of course with a man," Rosie cried, and since he made no comment, she proceeded to tell him all about it. "He had me to his place for dinner, a cozy little cabin in the woods. We had venison stew, and at first I thought I wouldn't be able to eat it because, although I was sitting in the kitchen, I was facing the living room, which is where all of his animal heads were hanging. Oh, did I tell you he's a hunter? But then I suggested we switch seats, and once I was facing the sink, the venison went down just fine. And afterwards, we went into the living room and put on an old Band album and pulled up the rugs and danced—"

"Rosie, are you making this up?" Frank interrupted.

"Of course not. Why would I do that? And I told him all about how you and I used to dance in the living room before you got so serious and decided that you didn't like rock and roll anymore, and he told me that that was the very same thing that happened with him and his wife...ex-wife, I should say. We had ourselves quite a time, Frank, drinking wine and dancing. And when I told him that I was planning to go to Europe for a year after the house is sold...Oh, did I tell you that I'm going to Europe?...Do you know what he said,

Frank? He said, 'I've never been to Europe, Rosie. You think about whether or not you'd like some company,' because he's self-employed, you see, and he can take off whenever he wants. And when I got home I lay in bed like a school girl going over everything he said, everything I said, wondering whether—"

"Rosie, is this some scheme to keep me from selling the house?"

Rosie looked at her watch. "Oh, Frank," she cried. "I have to go. I'll be late for work."

"Work? What work?" he grumbled, but Rosie, who abhorred tardiness, had no time to explain and no choice but to hang up the phone.

Rosie couldn't have been happier. The weeks that she had spent on the sofa seemed surrealistic now, like something that had taken place under water. It had never occurred to her that she might meet a man, a nice one, no less. The only thing that troubled her was that the Rosie that Les was…would it be too presumptuous to say 'falling in love with'?…was Rosie at her best, or Rosie in transition, or, to be perfectly honest, Rosie on Zakcor and as thin as a twig for a very good reason. She had already put back two pounds, and once the weight was back, the clothes wouldn't fit and the hair would look ridiculous. And God knows what would happen when she went off the Zakcor. She hadn't been to see Blanche again, but she knew the woman was scrupulous and she doubted that she would let her renew the prescription (which was only for three months) unless she could persuade her that she was still very depressed—which would be difficult under the circumstances. What she had to do, the next date for sure, was get Les to see that she had another side, that had she been under the influence of that other side the night at his cabin, she wouldn't have had the nerve to ask him to switch seats with her let alone to suggest that they pull up the rugs and dance. And if he had suggested it, she would have refused, too shy to consider hopping around the room with a stranger. She had put off her disclosure in the cabin, because, well, she had been having too much fun, but the next time, she would tell him. And if he didn't balk, why then, yes, of course, she'd love to have him come to Europe with her.

But Les was out of town for a few weeks, building an entertainment center for a family in Rochester, and by the time he got back, Rosie had met yet another man.

Phil Morris was a widower who lived on Rosie's block. He had a nasty dog, a big German Shepherd who frequently got away from him, and Phil, who otherwise kept to himself, could often be seen striding down the street with a red leash in his hand, hollering, "Reese! Reese, Come!"

It was a Sunday, and Rosie, who had had a bagel for breakfast, was at the sink rinsing the knife she had used to slice it when she saw Reese through the window. He was in her backyard, pulling at Jason's Frisbee, which had somehow got stuck in between the boughs of one of her azaleas. She opened the window and was just about to holler when she heard the dog's owner calling his name from out in front of the house. The dog stopped what he was doing and cocked his head pensively for a moment, and then, having reached a decision, went back about the business of trying to dislodge the Frisbee—with a vengeance now, growling and shaking his head, and thus the bush, from side to side. Then the next thing Rosie knew, her neighbor was in her backyard, pulling at the dog (who stopped pulling at the Frisbee long enough to snap at him), and trying to fasten the leash to his collar.

They had quite a struggle, but in the end Phil Morris won and was in the process of dragging Reese away when he happened to look up and see Rosie at the window. She smiled immediately and called out, "Beautiful day."

He stared at her with his mouth opened. Then his lips began to work. "Please tell Mrs. Campbell I'm terribly sorry about her azalea," he said.

Rosie's smile broadened. "Don't you recognize me?" she asked.

He stepped up closer to the window and squinted. "Mrs. Campbell?" he asked.

Rosie laughed. "I'm terribly sorry," Phil Morris said, and he hurried away.

An hour later the doorbell rang, and when Rosie went to answer it, she found Phil Morris standing on her stoop with a small azalea in a green plastic pot. "You didn't have to do that," Rosie said as she reached to receive his offering.

"I wanted to," he said, and since he didn't turn to go, Rosie invited him in for a cup of coffee.

Rosie knew nothing about Phil Morris except his name and, of course, his dog's name. But he, she realized soon enough, had learned a thing or two about her. He said that he had heard that she and Mr. Campbell had separated, and he wanted her to know that if she needed something repaired or had some other emergency that she didn't know how to deal with, he was at her service. "I know what it's like to find yourself alone and unable carry out the tasks that had previously been the specialty of your spouse," he said sadly.

Rosie laughed. "I was always the handy one," she confided. "Frank couldn't screw in a light bulb on his own."

"Oh, I'm terribly sorry. I didn't mean to suggest—"

"Mr. Morris, you must stop being terribly sorry about everything," she cried cheerfully.

He smiled uneasily, the corners of his lips vanishing behind the ends of his dark mustache, and Rosie realized that he was handsome—or would have been if not for his tick. (He had a odd habit of widening his eyes and blinking every few minutes, as if he wished to generate air flow under his lids.) Watching him, Rosie was suddenly curious to know how his wife had died, though she managed to refrain from asking. She had to watch herself these days. Since the advent of the Zakcor, she blurted things out even before she realized that she was thinking them. "What kind of work do you do, Mr. Morris?" she asked instead.

"Phil, please. And you're?"

"Rosie."

He went to extend his hand, but then, realizing that Rosie, at the other end of the table, was too far away to shake it without getting out of her seat, withdrew it and laughed nervously. "I'm in books," he said. "An agent."

"Is that so!" Rosie declared, and she proceeded to tell him about her own literary history. And Phil, who seemed to loosen up a bit when he learned that they had this in common, began to tell her about some of his recent projects. And when he mentioned the annual book fair in Frankfort, Rosie interrupted to say that she would be going to Europe as soon as the house was sold and that Frankfort would likely be one of her stops. That led them into a conversation about real estate market values, and when Rosie mentioned what Frank had listed the house for, Phil said that he was terribly sorry to be sticking his nose where it didn't belong, but it sounded to him as if Frank were handling the sale of the house as a distress sale, that they could surely get another ten or fifteen thousand dollars for a place as lovely as theirs. And then Rosie admitted that she had thought the very same thing but would never have challenged Frank on a subject about which he knew so much more than her. And so comfortable did she feel with the man that she was tempted to tell him about the Zakcor too, that had they set the price after the drug had taken effect instead of before, she would have surely told Frank how she felt.

In this way, two hours passed, and when Phil happened to glance at the clock and realized that he had taken up so much of her time, he was astounded and deeply apologetic. As Rosie followed him to the door, she explained that she had had no plans for the day and that she had enjoyed their conversation. He turned then, and the look on his face assured her that he was surprised to hear this; clearly, he did not think of himself as an entertaining fellow. "Well, you look remarkably well," he said, widening his eyes and blinking absurdly.

Rosie laughed. Phil blushed. "Not that you didn't look well before," he stammered. "I mean, you look well for someone who's been through— Oh, goodness, I can't seem to manage—"

"Phil," Rosie said so briskly that he jumped, "it's okay for you to notice. I lost a lot of weight. I couldn't eat after he left—"

"Yes, yes, I know about that—"

"I couldn't function, period. And then one day I got up and I realized that I'd lost all this weight, so I decided to change my hair and clothes and give starting my life over a try. I'm flattered you noticed.

Please don't feel badly about it."

Phil looked down at his feet. "I wish I knew how to do it myself. My wife…well, I'm coping, I suppose. But I've lost something." He looked up again, into her eyes. "Some spark, some vitality. I haven't changed my life; I'm just continuing on without her. It's very difficult."

He grasped the door knob and exhaled. "Well, it's been nice."

"Yes, it has," Rosie said. "And I hope you'll come again."

Phil's eyebrows rose. "For coffee?"

"For coffee, for conversation, for a glass of wine, whatever. If you get to feeling badly and you want some company, come on over. Just don't bring Reese."

Phil's expression was nearly ebullient. His mouth had opened, and his lips were working hard on a response. Finally, he achieved one. "Why, yes. Thank you. Why, yes, I will come by one of these days."

And as he went out the door, his shoulders shaking slightly with repressed laughter, Rosie had no doubt he meant it.

Rosie, who had never had two men interested in her at the same time in her entire life, was intoxicated with self-esteem, and the fact that she knew it to be merely temporary hardly mattered; her bliss was simply too intense to be contaminated by reflections on the trials of the past or uncertainties of the future. She was ablaze with love—for herself, for others, for Les, for Phil, for Frank even, for life itself! It was late Spring by then, and the sight of the buds that appeared on the trees, unfurling like fists that had long been clenched, was enough to bring her to her knees. There was a flower box outside the herbary, and one day as Rosie was about to enter, she heard a sound and turned to see a hummingbird hovering there. And the spectacle so overwhelmed her that she burst into tears and stood several minutes on the sidewalk sobbing vigorously into her palms while other pedestrians, unaware that a miracle had just transpired, glared at her as they walked on by.

When she crossed the street to have lunch at the diner now, her smile was so bright, so heartening, that the waitresses nearly knocked one another over in their attempt to get to her first, to have her sit at their station. And once she had been seated, the strangers surrounding her, discerning that there was something singular about the woman with the dangling earrings and the spiked hair, became more animated, spoke louder, as if for her benefit, and sometimes even attempted to include her in their conversations. Her friends, who had telephoned irregularly only to check on her, now pressed themselves on her greedily, insisting she find the time to see them, to hear them, to lift them up above the clouds, into spheres which they had no means of attaining on their own. If her window were open, the mailman, who had never said a word to her before, called in "Yoo hoo," before he went on his way. And the young couple in the ranch across the street, who had previously pretended not to notice Rosie as she came and went in the driveway, now took hold of their young daughter's arm and taught her to flap her hand in greeting.

Even Jason's attitude changed. He began to bring his friends around again. He insisted she tell them the story of Petey, and though it had appalled him the night he had first heard it, when she complied and told it again, he howled with laughter. They all did. There were tears in all of their eyes. They could hardly swallow the cookies that Rosie had set out for them or the milk that she had poured. And she told them other Petey and Frank stories too. Moribund Petey, dismal Frank. She told them about the delicious Caesar salad that she prepared one night, how a piece of Romaine had fallen from her plate and onto the floor, how Petey, who had seen it drop, had lifted his weight on his unsteady legs and come forward, how Frank, who was much too busy pontificating on the matter of some tedious law procedure that he had set into motion, didn't see Petey chewing, salivating, but in the end unable to swallow, how Rosie, who had the carpet to worry about, had picked up the discarded Romaine and set it on the edge of the table, how Frank, who had finally stopped talking and was now waiting for Rosie to comment (on his sagacity, no doubt), had looked into his plate, found it empty, espied the Romaine, and placed it into his mouth and swallowed with an ease that stunned Petey and Rosie both.

The boys hooted with laughter. Tom, the oldest, opened the door, gasping for air. Serious Frank, somber Frank; they could picture it. "Did you tell him?" asked Kurt, the one with the baseball cap, the one who had never met Frank. But the question was never answered, because the ones who did know him—and therefore knew very well that Rosie hadn't told him, the ones who knew very well what serious Frank's reaction would have been, who were, in fact, imagining it—had burst into fresh laughter.

Phil Morris came by again, with cut flowers this time, and a manila envelope tucked under his arm. He was terribly sorry to be such a pest, but he had received a manuscript from a young woman, and while he thought it suffered from first-time-out-overkill, he also thought it had some potential, and he wanted Rosie's opinion. Did she think she could take a look at a chapter or two? Did she think she could make the time?

Make the time? Why, that was what she was all about these days, making time—instead of killing it. She said that he should leave it with her, that she'd read it that night (why would she want to waste her precious time sleeping?) and that he could come by for both it and her opinion tomorrow. Could he bring some dinner? he wanted to know. Some Chinese food in cartons?

Les returned. He called in the morning to say that he had thought about Rosie the entire time he was away and couldn't wait to see her. He wanted to know if he could come by that night. Rosie explained that she had been asked to consult on a literary project and had already set aside that time to deliver her conclusion. Then the following night, Les pleaded. When he had picked her up to bring her to his cabin, she had come right out and he hadn't seen the house. Then, during the course of the evening, she had told him about the repairs that she had done to it. Now he wanted to come over and see for himself. "What a team we are!" he exclaimed. "Me a cabinet-maker and you so resourceful. Me a hunter, a sportsman, an outdoorsman, committed to sustaining myself with those edibles that God sets to wandering on my own ten acres, and you, a healer, an herbalist, scouring the earth—"

"Wait a minute," Rosie interrupted.

Les laughed, and Rosie could almost see his large, callused hand waving in the air in front of his furry face. "I know, I know," he said. "You're not an herbalist. You're just this fat old woman with a triple chin, and you can't dance either!" And he began to laugh all over again.

Phil arrived with a bag of Chinese food. He looked down at the coffee table, up at the dining room table in the adjoining room, and over towards the hall that led to the kitchen. "Where should I put this?" he asked.

"Wherever," said Rosie.

But Phil only continued to stand there, helplessly, in the middle of the living room. "I wanted to bring wine," he said apologetically. "But I was afraid that you'd think…Well, I don't want you to think that I'm moving too fast, pushing you into something that you're…Oh, dear. I'm not very good at this."

Rosie came forward, with the intention of taking the bag from him, but when she saw that his bottom lip had dropped and was quivering slightly, she changed her mind and leaned forward and kissed it instead. "Oh, my," said Phil when she pulled away, and he smiled, revealing his teeth for the very first time.

The innocent kiss, however, must have unbalanced Phil, for he floundered even more during their dinner—which they had on the coffee table—than he had on the occasion of their last meeting, and his tick was almost continuous. He had brought both white and fried rice, and he put a scoop of each into his plate, smiled, and then, picking up his fork, looked amazed to see that he had forgotten to add anything from the carton containing the pepper steak. Rosie passed it over to him, and in the process of spooning it out, he knocked the carton over. And then his hands, which were quaking, came up so fast to set the carton right that his elbow struck his water glass and its contents spilled. He looked up at Rosie, his brows furrowed and his thin lips pulled back so far in anguish that his mouth took on the appearance of an elastic band. "I don't know what's wrong with me," he lamented.

Rosie bounced up from the bean bag she had been sitting on and went into the kitchen. When she returned, she had a dishtowel, a bottle of plum wine, and two glasses. "Let me help you with that," said

Phil, but as he was getting up, his knee struck the coffee table, and though nothing more spilled, the cartons jumped and the plates and glasses all slid closer to Rosie's side. Phil sank back onto the sofa, emitted a groan of defeat, and covered his face with his palm. Once Rosie had set down the wine bottle and glasses and dabbed at the puddle of water, she reached across the table and gently detached Phil's fingers from his face. "Shall we talk about the manuscript?" she asked.

"I despise deviousness," Phil said flatly.

"Deviousness? I saw no evidence of that."

He sat forward again. "No, not in the manuscript. In people. In me. You see, I really only wanted to see you again. I lied when I said that I wanted you to look at the manuscript. I had already decided to reject it before I gave it to you. I just couldn't think of another way…And then last night, I was lying in bed, and I realized what a terrible thing I had done, giving you a thing like that to read, taking up your time…I've been dishonest. Forgive me."

Rosie reached up and patted her spikes. "I know how you feel," she said. "I've been feeling dishonest myself. Look at me! I met a man recently—" She stopped to register the look of disappointment that immediately flashed on Phil's face. "It was only one date," she went on quickly. "A nice fellow, like yourself. And all night long it was in my head that I should tell him that this isn't the real me—"

"But it is the real you," Phil said sadly. "I mean, it's true that you don't look quite the same as you used to, but unless he's a very shallow man, I'm sure it's your personality that attracted him to you."

"Perhaps, but you see, even—"

"Oh, I can see what you're trying to say. You're afraid that now that the crisis has passed, you'll put back the weight and that then he'll lose interest." He sighed deeply. "Well, I'm sorry to hear I have a competitor. Though I should have known, a woman like you. And let me say this, just on the off chance that it might sway you in your thinking." He reached out and touched Rosie's hand with his fingertips, looked at them in surprise, and quickly withdrew them again. "I've forgotten what I wanted to say," he said. He looked up at the ceiling, then down again. "No I haven't. There I go again. I wanted to say that I wouldn't care if you put the weight back on. What I like about you is the way you laugh, the fact that you're not afraid to say what you're thinking, your cheerfulness, your candor." He lowered his voice to a whisper and looked aside. "Like when you kissed me before."

Rosie was touched, and though all of the qualities that he had referred to were evident only by virtue of the Zakcor, she could not bring herself to ruin the moment by telling him so. She picked up the cellophane bag containing the egg rolls and placed one onto each of their plates. "Let's eat," she said cheerfully.

Les didn't knock when he came the next evening. He just opened the side door and yelled, "I'm here!"

Rosie heard him from Jason's room. She had been going from room to room, looking for photographs of her former self and carrying them into her bedroom to deposit them in the bottom drawer of Frank's bureau. She scanned the walls quickly, and satisfied to see nothing but heavy metal posters, she called out, "Coming," and ran down the stairs.

A sly smile appeared in the middle of the thicket that surrounded Les's mouth when he saw her, and from behind his back, a box of candy. "Got you a little gift," he sang.

"Oh, how sweet!" Rosie exclaimed, but as she went to take it from him, he caught her fingers and pulled her to him and began to hum and waltz her around the kitchen. "Have you thought anymore about Europe?" he asked.

"Les, this is our second date!" she cried happily, and she freed herself from his grip and went to check the water that was on the stove for the pasta she had promised to prepare.

"I like those pants," Les said, and when she turned, Rosie found him staring at her backside (he had spoken to it, actually), which she had squeezed into a pair of Jason's faded blue jeans. "The water's not ready yet," she said. "Shall we have the tour?"

They began in the basement, with Rosie showing him the water heater that she had installed some years back. Then they went up into the living room, where she described the fake brick wall that she had torn down and replaced with sheet rock. Les ran his hand along the wall, looking for seams. "You won't find any," Rosie said. "I spackled and sanded several times over before I painted." They went upstairs then, into Rosie's bedroom, and while Les looked around, she began a rather long-winded and well-rehearsed speech on the rewiring that she had done up there and the tile work that she had accomplished in the bathroom. For obvious reasons, she was nervous about having Les in her bedroom. Frank was the only man that she had ever slept with, and she thought she might not have minded becoming romantic with Les if Phil had not come into her life. Since she couldn't imagine having two lovers at the same time, she had decided not to have any for the time being. And as if he understood very well what she was trying to conceal with her lengthy dissertation on electricity and grout, Les came forward and put his arms around her. "We should hurry along," she said quickly. "The water's surely boiling by now."

Les stepped back. "Sorry," he mumbled, and he ran a finger under his nose. "It's just that you're so…so foxy."

"Come on," she said, and she took his hand and led him out of that room and into Jason's.

When she had shown the house to the potential buyers that had been by the week before, they had appeared startled when she opened the door to Jason's room. The woman had covered her mouth and the man had nodded his head as if to say, It's okay, we've seen enough. But Les seemed to be mystified by the sight of Jason's clothes lying in heaps on the floor and the heavy metal groups on the walls, some of whom had earrings in their nipples. "This room was unfinished when we moved in," Rosie said. "I had to do everything. Of course, it's difficult to see with all this clutter."

Les, who appeared not to be listening, moved forward, around the clothing heaps, until he was eye to eye with a savage-looking young man on the far wall. "Boys," he mumbled, and he moved to look at the poster beside it.

Rosie came in too. "We should hurry," she whispered. But Les was going from poster to poster now, looking at each with somber regard.

There was a tall shelf in the corner, on which, in addition to several books, Jason kept his extensive tape collection. Now Rosie noticed that there were some photographs there as well, which she had forgotten about when she had been up there earlier. Most of them were of girls, school pictures with signatures on the back. But there was also, Rosie realized with horror, a picture of the three of them, Frank and Jason and herself. She remembered it. It had been taken up in Maine, outside of the bed-and-breakfast that they had stayed in for a few weeks one summer. Rosie had given the camera to an old man they had met and asked him to take the picture, but he had snapped before Rosie had got back to the others. He caught her from the back, looking over her shoulder at him, her brows arched and her mouth opened in surprise, her double chin grossly evident. She was wearing shorts, and a sleeveless top that exposed her then-heavy upper arms. It was her aversion to the photo that had compelled Jason to insist on keeping it.

As it was, the left side of the picture, which was the part where Rosie was, was concealed by another photo—that of Jean Marie, the curly-headed girl whom Jason had dated over the previous summer. All that showed was Jason and Frank, who were standing side by side, Jason grinning and Frank pouting, with the bed-and-breakfast's porch behind them.

Les, who had completed his investigation of the last poster, now moved to stand in front of the shelf. "Pretty girls," he mumbled. "Lots of tapes. Must get it from his mother." And he turned suddenly to smile at Rosie, who quickly smiled back. "Oh, and this must be Jason," he said, lowering his head to look at him, and at Frank as well. Then his hand came up from his side, and for a second Rosie, who was holding her breath, was certain that he would pull the photo out from behind the other. But he only scratched his ear and then turned to follow her downstairs.

Luckily, Les had a job down in South Jersey in the morning, and so he couldn't stick around after dinner as long as he would have liked. He said it was a shame that he would have to drive north to get home only to have to pass through this way again to get to the job site, especially since he already had his work clothes and tools in his truck. But Rosie pretended to fail to grasp his intent and quickly got out of her chair to clear away the salad plates, and Les did not mention it again.

Afterwards Les, who said he was feeling his age that night, suggested they dance to something slower than what they had danced to last time, and Rosie found an Art Garfunkel in the album cabinet. Les was tall and well built and he hummed nicely, and while they were dancing, Rosie, who liked the feel of his whiskers on her cheek, began to think that maybe she should ask him to spend the night after all. Then she remembered the photo in Jason's room and changed her mind.

He kissed her though before he left, sweetly rather than passionately, an enduring kiss such as she had not had in a good many years. It nearly rendered her insensible. Her smile afterwards was both rapturous and moronic, the look of someone returning from a near-death experience, she imagined, but she had no control over the thing. And thus she was relieved when he drew back from her and she saw that his smile was just the same. "In a few days," he whispered, swaying slightly. He took her hand from her heart and placed it on his. "Thanks for dinner, Rosie Campbell."

"Thank you," she whispered back. "Thank you for coming, Lester Bakerson. And thanks for the flowers."

Les's dreamy expression vanished and his features began sliding every which way. "Flowers?"

Rosie opened her mouth and blinked at him. She was about to say, Why those flowers there, and turn him towards the vase on the end table when she remembered that the flowers had been from Phil, that Les had brought the candy. Godivas. Her favorite. They were still in the kitchen, up on the counter. She forced a laugh. "What am I thinking of? I meant the candy. Thanks so much for the candy."

But Les, who had been looking about the room, had seen the vase for himself now. He was staring right at it. He didn't say anything, but his expression revealed his unease, or perhaps something stronger than that. Rosie struck her head with her palm. "The flowers were from Jason," she said. "For Mother's Day."

Les brightened immediately. "You had me going for a moment," he said, and he embraced her once more before leaving.

Rosie had several calls in the morning while she was trying to get ready for work. First Les called, to say that he had had a really nice time and that he'd call her as soon as he was back in town. And he was so sweet on the phone, so sincere, that Rosie all but decided that she had better tell Phil Morris that she couldn't see him anymore when he, Phil, called. She had been thinking about him the night before when Les was over, wondering whether he would see Les's car in her driveway. He might even have taken Reese for a walk and seen them dancing to Art Garfunkel through the living room window. So she was not surprised to hear his voice, and she braced herself for the lament that she expected to follow. But Phil, who, in fact, sounded a good deal more cheerful than usual, only said, "Rosie, I've been dying to ask you this question. Do you play chess?"

Rosie did, or at least she used to. When she and Frank still lived in the city, Rosie had played regularly with an older woman who lived in their building. When the woman passed on, she tried to teach Frank to play, but his mood remained sour for hours on end after he lost, and eventually she put the board in the back of the closet where it would not be likely to remind Frank of his failures. "Why, yes," she said. "Why do you ask?"

"I'd like to invite you over to play a game with me tonight," Phil said. "I was up half the night thinking about it. Betty and I used to play, and since she died I haven't touched the board. This is a big step for me, Rosie. I'll fix us dinner, though I must tell you right now that I never learned to cook properly. I generally eat take-out or TV dinners myself, but I think I can manage something simple, maybe some steaks and a salad. What do you say?"

What could she say? "I'm afraid of Reese," she hedged.

Phil laughed, and Rosie realized that it was the first time she had ever heard him do so. "I'll put him in the basement. He won't mind. Do you know, he hasn't run away from me since the day I found him at your house. Since the day I found you! I think he planned it. I think getting us together was his intention all along. Oh, dear. I'm doing it again, making it sound as if…"

Rosie laughed heartily and asked what time he wanted her, and his brief hesitation before answering made her think that had he been on Zakcor, he might have said, "All the time" instead of, "Eight o'clock."

No sooner had she hung up the phone when it rang again, and her mirth was still in her voice when she answered. "Rosie, is that you?" asked Frank.

"Who else would it be? How are you doing?"

"I could be better, but never mind about that. What I wanted to tell you was that the people who looked at the house…What are you chuckling about?"

"Sorry," Rosie said. "It's just that you're so predictable and—"

"Rosie," Frank said firmly, "I'm in no mood for a confrontation."

That only made Rosie laugh harder. She held her hand over the mouthpiece so that he wouldn't hear.

Frank sighed and began again. "The people who looked at the house last week have made an offer, a handsome one, what we asked for, in fact. The only thing is that they would like to have the closing by the end of June. You see, they've got young children, and they want to be all settled in before the school year starts. Do you think you and Jason could find a place to live that quickly?"

"I told you, Frank, I won't need a place. I'm going to Europe. When the house is sold, I'll leave."

"Well, what about Jason then?"

"Jason will have to move in with you until he starts college in September."

"Rosie, I can't have him here."

"Why not?"

"It would be awkward. Sheila and I are working through a few problems and—"

"The boy is never home, Frank. He'd just need a place to sleep and a meal now and then—"

"But Rosie, you don't understand. This relationship is new—"

"What's to understand, Frank? I have a new relationship too. In fact, I have two of them."

"Two," he mumbled under his breath. "Last time it was one, now it's two. Next time it will be three, I suppose."

Rosie laughed abruptly. "Oh, I hope not, Frank. You have no idea how confusing this is. For instance, the one who came over for dinner last night brought me candy and the one who came over the night before brought me flowers, and when the one from last night was leaving, I got confused and—"

But her explanation was in vain; Frank had already hung up the phone.

Phil was smiling when he opened the door, and Rosie could not help but be pleased to think that she had made this difference in him. "Come in, come in," he said, sweeping his arm to show her the way.

The house was a split-level, a large one, and the rooms were spacious—or maybe they only seemed so because of the lack of clutter. The furniture, what little there was of it, was mostly oriental, and the paintings on the walls echoed that theme. He brought her into the dining room, where he had set out china and crystal and candles in tall brass holders on a chiffon tablecloth. The windows were opened, and the drapes, which were a pale pink linen, fluttered elegantly. This was not a room, nor a house for that matter, for rock and roll, Rosie mused, and she was in the process of deciding once more in Les's favor when Phil surprised her by stepping toward her, awkwardly, and kissing her, a quick peck on the side of the mouth. His smile, which followed immediately, was the smile of a little boy who had just done something that he hadn't been sure he was capable of doing, and Rosie couldn't help but be touched. "I'll be right back," Phil said, and no sooner had he left the room than Joni Mitchell's voice came wafting in. He had put on her "Blue" album, which Rosie rather liked. Then a moment later he entered from the kitchen with a platter in his hands. "Chateaubriand," he announced.

Rosie looked into the platter as he placed it on the table, at the perfectly seared steaks and the Château potatoes and the assorted vegetables and the sprigs of parsley, all wallowing in their pond of Sauce Béarnaise. "Why, Phil," she exclaimed, "you said you despised deception. You said you couldn't cook!"

"I never tried before. I didn't know. Why, really it's no more difficult than assembling a bicycle or anything else that comes with instructions. I found a cook book in the basement. It left nothing to be imagined. It even had a photograph." He widened his eyes and blinked several times.

"It's perfect," Rosie said, and for the first time since the advent of the Zakcor, she could think of nothing to add to that.

"Well, not quite," Phil confessed. "I had planned to make a salad too. I bought all the ingredients. But I didn't get the timing right. I prepared everything else first, and by the time I finished, it was far too late to begin on the salad. I'm sorry. I hope the salad wasn't something you were looking forward to too much."

Rosie laughed. It was clear that he really did hope that. She could imagine him in his office, struggling over the wording of his rejections letters, attempting, even as he explained the reasons for his disinclination, to inspire hope, lest anyone's feelings should be hurt.

He poured the wine, carefully turning the neck of the bottle so that not one drop would spill. "I have two things to tell you tonight," he said as he sat down. "I'm not ready to tell you just yet, but I wanted to tell you that I intend to tell you so that if I lose my nerve, you can remind me."

"Oh, tell me now. I can't stand suspense," Rosie cried, but when she saw how his face darkened just then, as if her entreaty necessitated full submission on his part, she reached out her hand and patted his and whispered, "It's okay."

The meal could not have been better if it been cooked by Escoffier himself, and Rosie ate more than she had at any time since her slumber in hell (which was how she now thought of that period when she had been so depressed). And the conversation was as rich and smooth as the wine. They talked about books for a good long time and found out that they had many favorites in common. Then, after a long discussion about the maternal anxieties of Virginia Woolf's Mrs. Ramsay in *To the Lighthouse*, the subject turned to children, who Phil professed to love though he and Betty had never had any of their own. They had tried, he said, but Betty had had some problems, and there had been several miscarriages. He asked about Jason, and to Rosie's surprise, he laughed heartily, with his hand up in front of his mouth as though his laughter embarrassed him, when she described some of Jason's antics over the years. Then Phil excused himself and went into the kitchen with the dinner plates and returned with a doily-covered sterling silver tray on which there sat two identical Tartelettes aux fruits. Rosie, who had not allowed herself a single dessert since her weight loss, felt her mouth watering instantly. She followed the descent of the tray with a greedy eye and wondered how far Phil had had to drive to find a French bakery. The pastry cases were a golden brown and perfectly formed. In each there were two pear halves encircled by glacé cherries, and the whole of it was smothered with an apricot glaze on top of which was angelica. "Wherever—?" Rosie began, but when she looked up and saw how he was beaming, saw the tears that glistened in the corners of his eyes, she knew the answer. "You made these?" she whispered.

Too choked up to answer, he merely nodded, and they had their dessert in a silence that was as exquisite as the Tartelettes themselves.

At Phil's insistence, they left the dishes where they were and adjourned to the den, where the chess board was all set up and waiting on a small oak table between two black leather club chairs. Beyond it was a sofa, covered in a coarse red, yellow, and black plaid fabric, and off to the side, a large oak desk on which several manuscripts were piled. This room was very unlike the rest of the house, and Rosie wondered whether Betty had decorated it as a concession to Phil's taste, or whether Phil had done it himself. She was about to ask when she remembered that Phil had two things to tell her, and so she asked about that instead.

They had brought a second bottle of wine in with them, and they sipped as they began their opening moves. "The first thing," Phil said softly, "concerns something that I want you to know about me. The second concerns something that I want to know about you." He kept his eyes on his pieces as he spoke, and Rosie surmised that here, at least, on the chess board, Phil would be aggressive, and not the least bit apologetic in the event that he should win. She pushed a pawn, and at the risk of losing his positional advantage, Phil took it. "I may have had an UFO encounter," he said matter-of-factly, and briefly his gaze lifted from the board. Ever polite, he waited until she had thought out and then made her move before continuing. "Thank you for not laughing," he went on. Then he moved his knight out, and Rosie, who was feeling the effects of the wine, realized that her bishop was in jeopardy. "I told a friend once, a colleague of mine, and he laughed, I'm sorry to say. He made quite a big deal of it, telling others in the office and making jokes. I couldn't blame him really. It was just the sort of thing you read about in those paperbacks in the supermarket. In fact, a few weeks before it happened, I had received just such a manuscript…and promptly rejected it. I thought it was a lot of nonsense, and if I had any interest in it at all, it was with the lunatics…or that's how I thought of them at the time…who professed to have had these encounters rather than with the encounters themselves." He stopped to take a deep breath, and, alas, to capture Rosie's bishop.

"Betty and I were staying up in the Catskills at the time. We had a little spat after dinner our last night there, and I decided to go for a walk. There was no one around. We weren't at one of those resorts up there, just some little inn on some lake. And I was looking into the lake when I saw this light, like a fire just under the surface of the water. I realized that it had to be a reflection and looked up. And there was this…this…thing. It had one very bright light in the center and a circle of smaller ones all around. It was just hovering there, noiselessly. I had no idea what it was, but it never occurred to me that it might be an alien spaceship because, well…I didn't believe in such things! I was scared, however, and I returned to our room immediately—or at least I thought that was what happened.

"I found Betty crying, and so angry that when she turned and saw me at the door, she took the shoe that she had been about to put on and threw it at me." He pointed to a tiny hairless area in his eyebrow. "See? I still have the scar. Now the argument that we'd had was nothing, some conflict about whether or not we would stop on the way home the next day to visit Betty's parents—certainly nothing that would warrant the weeping and the assault. And I said so. And Betty, who clearly would have been screaming if not for the fact that we were in an inn, cried, 'How could you leave me like this? On our vacation?' Well, to make a long story short, I had been gone four hours according to Betty, while, in my recollection, I had been gone all of ten minutes." He laughed, fondly, Rosie thought, and stretched his eyes. "Since then, I've had some very strange dreams, which I'd really rather not go into just now. And once or twice I even woke up with my nose bleeding, just like they do in the books. I thought you should know."

"Did Betty come to believe you? About the encounter?" Rosie asked.

Phil moved his queen to a position of greater advantage and waited until Rosie's rook had skated out to protect her own queen. "No. In fact, she insisted that I had made off with one of the waitresses. She even thought she knew which one it was. And she threatened to divorce me if I didn't own up to my misdeed. In the end I agreed that I had been out with the girl, the one she remembered from the dining room...though I didn't remember her myself. I said I had run into her just outside the inn and that we got to talking and she wound up walking with me half way around the lake. I said we discussed the problems that she was having with her boyfriend and that I suggested an approach that might mollify him over the matter of her misdeed, and that then she had gone off to try it and I had gone the rest of the way around the lake alone."

Rosie laughed. "That must have been difficult," she said. "I mean, if Betty's anything like...sorry...was anything like I am, she must have wanted specifics, the details about this conversation about the waitress's boyfriend."

Phil looked up with a twinkle in his eye. "Actually, the only difficulty was the lying, though not lying would have cost me my marriage. The waitress's relationship with her boyfriend required no invention on my part at all. You see, I had just read a manuscript concerning such a thing. It was fresh in my head. I'm not that imaginative. I wouldn't have been able to come up with something like that otherwise, especially in the state I was in, with Betty threatening divorce and the four hours that I couldn't account for...Oh, by the way, checkmate."

Rosie and Phil moved into the living room, where he now put on a Lou Reed album that she had never heard before. Beyond Lou's seductive biddings, she could hear Reese whining in the basement. "I should go," she said. "It must be very late."

"Don't go yet," he whispered, but he cocked his head, and she knew that he had heard Reese too.

"Why did you tell me?" she asked. "About your encounter?"

"I thought you should know. If you're going to conclude that I'm a flake, I'd rather you did so now, before…" He put his head back against the cushion and sighed up at the ceiling.

Rosie leaned in toward him. "Before what, Phil?"

He turned his head toward her but did not lift it. "I like you very much," he whispered.

"I like you too," she said, but as Reese was getting louder by the moment, she sat forward and clapped her palms on her thighs. "I'm leaving. He'll need to go out or something, won't he?"

Phil stared at her a moment longer, then he sat forward as well. "Yes. Come on. I'll walk you home."

"I drove," she said, and she pecked his cheek. And although Reese was barking now, she added, "But I'm not leaving until you tell me the other thing, the one that concerns me."

Phil stood up and pressed his lips together. He looked in the direction of the barking and then back at Rosie again. Then he took a deep breath and stated his query on the exhale. "I was wondering whether you'd meet me at the book fair in Frankfort." He removed his hands from his pockets and, wringing them, went on hastily. "I spend that part of every year in Europe, and I was hoping, since you're going to be there anyway, that we could spend it together." He reached down suddenly and touched a trembling fingertip to Rosie's upper lip. "Think it over. You don't have to tell me now. In fact, I'd rather you didn't. We've had such a lovely evening and I'll be so disappointed if you feel you must say no, for whatever reason…."

He slipped his hands back into his pockets and walked her to the door. But when she turned to face him there to say good-night, she noticed the activity in his pockets and nearly laughed, for it was as if he was trying to pull his hands free while his pockets sought to hold them fast. Finally, they escaped, halted uncertainly, and then found their way around her waist. He held her loosely at first, and at some distance. But then he inched forward and embraced her properly. He didn't kiss her, but his hold was surprisingly firm, urgent almost, and in spite of Reese's petitions, it was a good long time before he let her go again.

And so it went for the next few weeks—with the real estate closing fast approaching, all the sorting and packing and selling and storing yet to be done, Jason preparing for his graduation (he wanted no parties, thank God) and his move to his father's, and Rosie unable to decide whether she wanted to travel with Les or alone and then meet up with Phil in Frankfort.

She loved them both, was the problem. Or rather, she thought she loved whoever it was she was with at the time. And the juggling put some strain on her. The incident with the candy was not the only time that she confused one's largess with the other's. Les told her she had eyes like a cat's one night, and the following evening, when she and Phil were watching the little league game at the park, a cat went by, and Rosie said, "I don't think my eyes look like hers at all!" On another occasion, Rosie wore a blue dress to meet Phil at Giovanni's, an Italian restaurant midway between their houses, and when he commented on how "foxy" she looked in it, she said he hadn't said a thing about it the last time she'd worn it, though of course he had never seen it before.

It was easier to recover from these blunders with Phil, since she had been wise enough to let him know early on that he had a competitor. Whenever she fumbled, he looked aside with his lips pressed together, nodded his head, and when he looked back at her, he was smiling again, smiling and blinking wildly, trying his best to put the incident by. With Les it was more difficult. His eyes would narrow, and Rosie, who had come to understand that this was a signal that she had made an error, would feel compelled to explain it away with a lie. Unlike Phil, and fortunately, she was imaginative, and usually able to invent something on the spot. But afterwards, Les, who, though not as clever as Phil wasn't stupid either, would sulk and glance at her reproachfully until her suggestion ("Come on, let's dance," or "Come on, let's eat") would rouse him from suspicion's grip.

Since she couldn't decide who she best loved, she attempted to make her decision by determining who best loved her, but this proved an equally formidable task. Les swore that he couldn't get through an hour without her popping into his heart—though somehow Rosie didn't believe that it was his heart that was most apt to respond to the thought of her. He had gotten aggressive of late, was always pulling her toward him for a kiss, clinging to her after the music had stopped, running his hands down her arms or his fingertips under her chin. Frequently, he spoke to her breasts, and once he even winked at them. Thus far, she had gotten around what she knew very well to be his ultimate intention by meeting him in public places. He couldn't come to her house, she said, because Jason, who he'd never met, was having some trouble with the fact that his mother was dating and she didn't want to cause him any undue stress now that he had so much else to deal with, what with the move to his father's and the prospect of college looming just ahead. And with the packing up of the house to be completed and Rosie still working at the herbary, she needed her sleep and his place was so far away.

Phil, on the other hand, didn't verbalize his feelings for her, but that they existed was evident. He had found her an out-of-print book that she had been wanting and left it on her doorstep along with one long-stemmed red rose. He had taken a great liking to cooking now that he had begun, and once when she couldn't see him, because she had forgotten that Les had bought tickets for a Knicks game that night, he delivered the tournedos de boeuf that he had hoped to share with her to her house, and she and Jason (who thought it was "cool" that his mother had two boyfriends) ate it standing at the kitchen counter. He wasn't much of a kisser (their lips met, but never more than that), but his prolonged farewell embraces, which Rosie thoroughly enjoyed, had become something of a ritual.

And then there was the future to consider. Sure, Rosie had warned Les, but it was clear that he didn't really believe her story about actually being fat. She had gained back six pounds by now, and all the stylish clothes that she had charged to Frank's accounts were becoming a little tight on her. (There were times when she thought that Phil had taken up French cooking purposely, so that she would get fat faster and he would find himself sans competitors.) Les mentioned Europe every time he saw her. He'd even gone to an agency and gotten some brochures. What he wanted most, he claimed, was to go dancing with her in Paris. But Rosie wanted to start off in London, and then have a tour of the Lake District, and by the time she got to Paris, she might very well be right back to her former size! Would he want to dance with her then?

Phil didn't dance, but then if she were to meet him in Frankfort, it would be for the book fair and not the night life. He didn't mention it often—in fact, it was more often Rosie who brought up the prospect of their rendezvous—but he had indicated that he intended to stay in Frankfort for awhile. He wanted to visit some of the historical sites, particularly those that involved Goethe, who had been born there. He was rereading Goethe in preparation for it. He could do his work, he said, just as well in another country as he could in his office; his colleagues would simply mail him his authors' manuscripts and any others they thought he'd be interested in. In fact, he had one manuscript, a historical novel based on the "Sigurth" legend, which he thought a German publisher might find very attractive.

Rosie took all this to mean that he was prepared to stay on with her for as long as she would have him. And she believed that he, unlike Les, would love her fat or thin. But she had never gotten around to telling him about the Zakcor (he took such stock in honesty and she was afraid such an admission at this time would constitute deceit), and now she wondered whether he would love her still if she lost her candor. Would she lose her candor? Maybe she wouldn't, and then all this worrying would have been in vein. She might be fat and candid in Frankfort, and if that was case, then Phil was definitely the one to be with. But then again, she might be fat and insipid, in which case it would be better to be with Les in Paris, because certainly her chances of losing weight again for a disgruntled Les were greater than those of regaining her openness…or were they?

"I'm surprised to see you," Blanche said, and though her voice was as soft as ever, Rosie thought she detected some resentment in her tone.

"I've run out of pills," Rosie said flatly. "If I remember correctly, when you prescribed them you said that the effects would linger for three weeks once I was off them. So I've got to start right back on them again so that there won't be much of a gap. I'm terribly sorry for waiting until the last moment like this—" She hesitated, mildly amused to hear herself sounding like Phil. "—but I've been so busy, with the move and all…"

"Sit down," ordered Blanche.

Rosie was in a hurry, but as the last thing she wanted to do was annoy the other woman, she lowered herself to the edge of the sofa.

"You look wonderful," Blanche said unenthusiastically. "In fact, you look better than the last time you were here. You were a little too thin then, I thought. How do you feel?"

"Just terrible. That's why I need the pills."

Blanche brightened. "Ah. You've had a problem readapting to the work-a-day world. I knew it."

"No," stated Rosie, she hoped not indignantly. "That's not it at all."

"What then?"

Rosie sat back then and told her everything, all about the two men whom she was in love with and who were in love with her and wanted to be with her in Europe and how she often confused the things that one said and did with the things the other said and did, and how she had only a very short time left to make a decision, and then there were all the household items to make decisions about as well—in short, that with all this thinking and thinking, she was afraid she might be losing her mind.

Blanche nodded for a long time, so that Rosie thought she must be cultivating a solution. Finally she said, "I should have such problems."

Rosie got up and began to pace, her hands flying up from her sides. "You don't understand, Blanche. It was fun in the beginning, but isn't anymore. Phil knows about Les, but Les doesn't have a clue about Phil. If Phil calls to ask me out, I need only say that I had something else planned, and there are no questions asked. But even so, I feel so…so guilty all the time. And if Les calls on a night that I've planned to see Phil, why, I find myself making up the most outrageous things. And don't suggest that I just come clean, because I've considered that; I just can't do it. Because then I'd have to explain that I was seeing Phil from the beginning, and then Les would surely go away, and I haven't decided yet, and I don't know what to do."

Blanche smiled, sardonically, Rosie thought. "I had a girl in here a few hours ago, a sixteen-year-old with the very same problems."

"Blanche, please don't make light of this."

Blanche sat forward, her eyes narrowed, the set of her mouth tightening until it was no more than a smudge on her face. "Rosellen Campbell, Zakcor will not help you make any decisions. That's not its purpose. I can see I made a mistake by putting you on it in the first place, especially since it's still more or less in an experimental stage. Had I known that you only wanted it so that you'd be less of an introvert and therefore able to seduce—"

"Seduce!" Rosie interrupted. "It was never my intention to—"

Blanche stood up, and Rosie was surprised to see how short she was. "And it was never my intention to create a Jezebel."

"A Jezebel! Well…"

The two women stared at each other, defiantly. Then Rosie, who saw that her cause was hopeless, picked up her bag and went out the door.

One day during the week that followed Frank came by, with several chumps and a moving van apparently, and took away all those household items that he felt were rightfully his. When Rosie returned from work, she found the house half empty and a long note listing every article that he had taken and his justification for taking it. She was disappointed; she wished he'd taken everything. She had called once to inquire about renting storage space, but she had never gotten around to making the arrangements. The task of separating those things she wanted from those she did not was simply overwhelming; she didn't know where to begin.

At the counter in the kitchen she opened the newspaper and found an ad in the classified section for a company that professed to buy anything and everything. She was so distraught over this matter of Les and Phil that she had to read it three times before she could make sense of it. The notion of selling everything, all at once and for one price, was tempting, but instead of making the call she put the paper aside and dialed her friend Lois's number. She told her basically the same thing that she had told Blanche, that the task of deciding between the two men, along with the rest of it, was causing her to lose her mind. But Lois, who had had two one-night stands in the twelve years that she had been divorced, only laughed. "Come on, Rosie," she said. "Do you really expect me to sympathize?"

Jason came home from school, and when he saw the condition of the house, he went from room to room whispering things like "Cool" and "Awesome". There was a party that night, at his friend Tom's house, but now Jason wanted to know if they could have the party at his house instead, if Rosie would mind if they took what was left in the living room and stacked it all in one corner so that Tom's band could set up there and people could dance. Rosie, who was frantically leafing through her address book, looking for someone who might be able to advise her on the concerns of her heart, or at least empathize with her, said she didn't care.

She called her friend Elizabeth, the librarian she had once worked with, and told her about her travails. But Elizabeth, who said she'd give anything in the world to be in Rosie's shoes after being married to the same man for twenty-two years, only laughed. She called three other friends, and they all had a similar response. Wild with frustration, she began to call acquaintances, women who, during her brief association with bliss, had given Rosie their numbers and suggested they get together some day. But although most of this group listened politely while Rosie went on and on describing the details of her dilemma, in the end they all agreed that Rosie should be as happy as a lark.

She dialed one of the waitresses from the diner across the street from where she worked, but the line was busy. She was in the process of looking up another number when the phone rang. It was Phil, calling to find out what time she was coming over that night. "I'm terribly sorry," Rosie said, and again she was amazed to realize that she was beginning to sound just like him, "but I have to cancel for tonight. I have so many things on my mind. I wouldn't be able to concentrate on the game. I hope you didn't put yourself out too much over dinner," she added, though she knew very well that he had.

"Don't worry about it," Phil said. "The dinner, that is. Moules marinière is something I can polish off by myself. But if you want to talk…if I can be of any help…you sound terrible, Rosie. I wish there was something I could do."

Rosie was so touched that she made a hasty decision, and instead of calling Paula, a woman she'd met the last time she'd been to have her spikes trimmed, she called Les. Her heart was pounding furiously by the time he answered, on the ninth or tenth ring. "Rosie," he cried when he heard her voice. "Why, I didn't expect to hear from you tonight. I thought you had one of those literary sermons or whatever they are to present. My brother's here with his kids. We were about to go out for some Italian. Why don't you meet us. Why don't you bring Jason. If he met me, well, maybe then he wouldn't be so—"

"Les," she interrupted, "I don't know how to say this, but I'm thinking I should go to Europe alone."

She held her breath during the long silence that followed, for Les had a vengeful side. Once, for instance, he described with some glee his response to a wedding invitation that he had received from a former lover. He had sent the woman a note explaining that he was still too dispirited over the way their relationship had ended to attend, but he typed it in such a way that the letters that appeared on the vertical crease spelled out their own profane message. Rosie expected to hear a similar edict now, but when his voice, which was grainy with defeat, finally came, all he said was, "I should have known."

"I'm so sorry," Rosie whispered, and as Les made no response, she quietly hung up the phone.

In the next five minutes Rosie experienced many emotions, the first of which was profound relief; for better or worse she had made a decision. She dialed Phil, eager to tell him that yes, she would be happy to meet him in Frankfort, but as it happened, Phil was out. She got his answering machine instead, and when she heard his tediously articulate drone on the tape, the pauses between sentences and even between numbers as he confirmed the sequence the caller had dialed (as if he thought the caller might be mentally disabled!), she came to think she had made a very grave error by rebuffing Les like that.

Now she felt that she must call Les back immediately, let him know that she had not put the notion of traveling with him to rest after all. Otherwise she would never see him again. Dear Les, with his animal heads and his expansive rock and roll collection. What had she been thinking of? But she was so distracted, standing against the wall with eight of her ten fingers on her lips, that she had failed to see Jason come forward to take up the phone. "Hurry," she said, but Jason, who was explaining to Tom about the condition of the house and its suitability for the party, only waved his hand at her.

She chewed on her knuckles and considered that this new hitch, Jason having taken over the phone, might be a sign that she had better leave things as they were. In the meantime, and in spite of the insight, the names of the two men and their attributes continued to bounce from one side of her head to the other, like a Ping-Pong ball between the paddles of two ruthless players—Les, Phil, Les, Phil, Rock and Roll, books and food, drama and sex, conversation and affection. And as if she were one of the players and not a mere spectator to this mental tournament over which she had no control, she began to pant, and when she came back into awareness, she realized that Jason was now in the living room, stacking end tables in a corner. She dialed Les, with the intention of hanging up as soon as she heard his voice, for she simply had to hear it one last time. But his hello confirmed that he had been crying—a grown man, a hunter! crying over her!—and thus she broke down and, crying herself, said his name and then he said hers and then they were laughing and crying simultaneously, and she was telling him that yes, she would reconsider, that she was terribly sorry to have upset him, that she didn't know what was wrong with her, but whatever it was, it had nothing to do with him. And she was just about to tell him that she would meet him and his brother for Italian as well when she happened to look out the window and see Phil going by with Reese. As the drapes were gone (Frank, of course), he was able to see her too, and he smiled and waved. And Rosie, who was holding the receiver away from her ear, oblivious to the voice that was coming from it, recalled with a gasp that she was responsible for that toothsome smile, bright against the darkening sky, that she had coaxed it out from the depths of Phil's soul, and now she felt that she had made a huge mistake by calling back Les.

The teenagers began to arrive, with cigarettes and six packs, and before Rosie knew what was happening, the house filled up with smoke. Jason had left only the sofa in place in the living room, and there were eight or nine girls squeezed together on it, passing around what Rosie hoped was yet another cigarette and giggling their frizzy-haired heads off. She went back to work with her telephone book, and when she realized she had finished with all her acquaintances, she began calling her friends for a second time, trying to get someone to see that she was genuinely in need of help. She was on the phone with Elizabeth when the band started up, and even though the music was grievously loud, she was able to hear the librarian laughing through the receiver.

She was sobbing when she hung up, and as she couldn't bear the thought of these blithe young people seeing her in such a state, she decided that she must leave the house at once. She seemed to remember having had her car keys in hand when she went to bring in the mail, and thus she thought to look for them first on her desk. But apparently the desk and the other den furniture had been Frank's, for when she went in, she found the room entirely empty. She ran from room to room after that, frantically checking all remaining surfaces.

Then, on a whim, she opened the front door and stuck her hand into the mailbox. The keys were there, sure enough, along with the mail, and she was about to leave with both when she realized that her driveway was full of cars; there was no way she would ever get hers out. With the intention of stifling the moan that she felt emerging, she lifted her hand to her face, but before it could make contact with her mouth, which was drooping with anguish, someone grabbed it and pulled her back into the house. She turned to find Hank, the tallest of Jason's friends, looming over her, saying, "Wanna dance, Mrs. Campbell?"

She freed herself and ran out again, heading the way Phil had gone. She had to tell someone about her dilemma, someone who would understand, and she thought Phil might be the one. She had reached the corner and was heading out towards the highway when she realized that Phil was a part of her dilemma, fifty percent in fact, and that it would be entirely inappropriate for her to speak to him about it. She kept on walking nonetheless, and an hour later she found herself in front of Shop Rite, where she leaned against the glass and scanned the faces of the shoppers within hoping to detect one who was at least vaguely familiar to her. Then she turned to look over those who were loading groceries into their cars in the lot, but they were all strangers too. It began to drizzle, and Rosie, who was wearing a cotton sun dress, took shelter in the store.

It was very bright in Shop Rite, and knowing that her face must be puffy and tear-streaked, she hung her head as she went up one aisle and down the next. She thought making a purchase would make her look less suspicious, but she remembered she had no money on her. She was on her way back out again when she happened to catch the eye of a woman who was coming in. The woman made the mistake of smiling at Rosie, and as soon as the automatic door opened, Rosie approached her, saying, "I must talk to you, please."

The woman had an angelic face, or so it seemed to Rosie, clear blue eyes, a nose that was slightly hooked, and a weak little chin made more evident by her vigorous gum-chewing. As if she were used to being accosted by strangers, she allowed Rosie to take her elbow, turn her around, and guide her out the exit door. Rosie began her narration immediately, though the woman, whose name was Dolly, seemed to be more interested in the fact that she was getting wet, for she stood with her purse above her head, her gaze sweeping the charcoal firmament, her chin rotating wildly now. "Let's sit in my car," she suggested when Rosie finally stopped to catch her breath.

Dolly, who was about Rosie's age, had an old Chevy, and there was a lot of stuff in its back seat. Rosie was too upset to do more than glance at it, but she did note the platinum blonde wig among the clothing and the trash bags and the empty soda bottles. She settled herself in the passenger seat, and as soon as Dolly had gotten in on the other side, she continued from the point at which she had left off. Dolly seemed to listen earnestly now, her green eyes, which were enhanced by the dark circles beneath them, shifting back and forth between Rosie's for a good half hour. When Rosie was finally done, Dolly said, "Let's pray."

"What?" asked Rosie.

Dolly turned her palms upward, and closed her eyes. "God," she began, tilting her head toward the roof of the car. But then she bent her head and opened her eyes again, and seeing that Rosie was prepared to be no more than a spectator, took hold of Rosie's hands and turned them upward, and to keep them from caving in, slid her own palms beneath them.

Her prayer was nearly as long as Rosie's narration had been, and twice as repetitive. On and on she went, breathlessly, beseeching first God, and then His various cohorts, to have mercy on Rosie, to bless "this poor, miserable creature who is clearly in so sorry a state," to forgive her for being tempted to play with the hearts of men (the word "men," Rosie noted, she pronounced with some disdain) and to give her the wisdom to make the decision that would best enhance her future.

While she petitioned, Rosie looked out the window, embarrassed to be seen with a clearly-praying stranger in an old, dented Chevy. But the rain fell harder, and as she saw no one she knew (in fact, the lot was nearly empty now), eventually she lifted her head and mumbled a few words on her own behalf. Perhaps God didn't want to hear from her though, for just then there was a thunderous roar, accompanied by a flash of lightening.

Dolly ceased praying and lowered her head, but she kept her eyes closed for some moments longer. Then, all at once, she cocked her head, so that Rosie assumed that she was listening for God's response. Then she smiled, so that now Rosie thought that God was responding, jovially, as her friends had all done. In the hope of hearing for herself, she inclined her head toward Dolly's ear, but she heard nothing. Finally Dolly opened her eyes and withdrew her hands from Rosie's. "Do you feel better?" she asked.

"Yes," Rosie lied.

Dolly turned away from her, rolled down the window, removed her wad of gum and flicked it out, and set about lighting a cigarette. Her brown hair was streaked with gray, Rosie noticed, and poorly cut. Her nostrils were long and arched. She exhaled smoke through them and turned back toward Rosie. "You know," she said in a voice that sounded harsh after her praying one, "if I were you, I'd go to Europe by myself, leave them both behind in the dust."

"No, you don't understand," Rosie began. "This thing that's happened to me, it's kind of like the Cosmic Soup. You know, all the ingredients being just right at exactly the right moment for life to begin?" She hesitated, for it occurred to her that such a notion might seem blasphemous to a woman as prayerful as Dolly. But Dolly was staring out the window now, puffing out smoke rings and looking at the lightening flashing in the distance. "You see what I'm saying?" Rosie went on. "This could only happen once. It was a fluke—the weight loss, the Zakcor...If I reject them both, no one may ever be interested in me again."

"So?" Dolly queried.

When the rain abated, Rosie thanked Dolly and took to the streets again, walking up and down them as she had the aisles in the supermarket. She was still carrying the mail that she had removed from the box at her house, and when she realized that, she stuck the batch into a corner mailbox and went on her way without it. It was very late when she finally got home, and except for hers and Jason's, there were no cars in the driveway or out in the street. She found Jason asleep on the sofa, on his back, snoring loudly, and with one arm dangling. There were a few beer cans here and there, and one cigarette burn in the carpeting, but little else to show that a storm of teenagers had blown through. Rosie bent over Jason and gently kissed his forehead. Then she went to the counter and found the newspaper that she had been looking through several hours earlier. There were glass rings on it now, and what looked to be a salsa stain, but the ad was still legible. Rosie dialed and left a message on the company's answering machine, stating her name and number and that she wanted the contents of her entire house sold. She was just about to head up the stairs for bed when the phone rang.

She jumped, and although she didn't want it to awaken Jason, she let it ring five times before she finally mustered the nerve to answer. "Hello," she said curtly, and she decided immediately that whoever it was (and he had to have some nerve to call so late) would be the one that she would reject.

"Rosie?" the male voice said. "Oh, Rosie, Rosie, Rosie."

"It's three o'clock in the morning, Frank! Have you been drinking?" she cried shrilly.

"Yes, indeed I have."

"Whatever can you want at this hour?"

"I'm thinking of canceling the closing, Rosie."

"Well, then, fine. Cancel it."

"You mean to say you wouldn't mind?"

"Not as long as you give me half of the money we would have received."

"Oh, Rosie, Rosie, Rosie. You're missing the point. I'm going to give you something of much more value than half the money, the thing I took from you, my poor Rosie. Me, specifically. I miss you so. I don't know what I ever thought I'd accomplish, moving in with a beautiful young thing with whom I have nothing in common. I want you, Rosie. I want your stability. I want—"

"I'm not stable anymore, Frank," she cried.

"Come on, Rosie, you're the most stable woman I know, the Rock of Gibraltar. Don't put yourself down like that."

"No, I'm not, Frank, I'm a Jezebel."

"I reduced you to that, to all those lies you've been telling me. The men, the trip…Can you ever forgive me? I don't know what I was thinking of when I left you. I want to put my arms around you, Rosie. I want to feel your bulk—"

"My bulk is gone, Frank!" Rosie screamed.

"Rosie, this is me, Frank, your husband. Let's be—"

"No," she shouted, and adding an expletive such as she imagined Les had employed in his cryptic note to his ex-girlfriend, she slammed down the phone.

Rosie was on a train. She had already been to London and was now on her way to the Lake District. She had a novel opened on her lap, though she wasn't reading it. The man across the aisle had smiled at her earlier, and she had a feeling that if she looked in his direction again, he would begin a conversation. In preparation for such an event, she had been concentrating on being candid, on saying whatever came into her head. But of course her imaginings of the various conversations that might ensue had already put the possibility of candidness by. The man looked to be a few years older than her, gray, clean-shaven, and sensible-looking in his black trench coat. He had a newspaper, but he wasn't reading either. She could see with the corner of her eye that his chin was lifted, that his head was inclined in her direction. Thinking that he might speak whether she looked at him or not, she made a decision and put her head back against the headrest and closed her eyes.

She had been a little lonely at first, especially dining out. But her third week in London she had met a woman, a wonderful woman who sold insurance by day and did physic healings in the evenings, and they had done some shopping together and gone to the theater on four occasions. She had also looked up an old college buddy, an exchange student who had often copied her homework assignments. He owned a travel agency now, and he and his wife, who worked for him, had provided Rosie with some sound traveling tips and several home-cooked meals as well. In the end she had had a ball in London. She had even made some notes, and if her successive stops turned out to be equally interesting, she thought she might try to write a travelogue when she got back home—if she had the time. Gail, who Rosie had left scouting for a larger shop, had promised Rosie her job back when she returned. Les and Phil and Frank had all promised to wait, and in the meantime to write. She had told all three, graciously, of course, that they needn't bother, on the matter of the former at least, but they had professed their undying devotion and insisted they would do so nonetheless.

Jason popped into her head, and she remembered that he was starting school today, his first day of college. She had sent him the address of the inn that she would be staying at in the Lake District, and she thought it likely that there would be mail for her upon her arrival. Then, all at once and out of nowhere, she recalled that this was in fact the very day on which she had once planned to kill herself, and she laughed abruptly. Realizing how obtrusive her blast had been in the otherwise quiet car, she opened her eyes and caught the stranger staring at her. He looked away, then changed his mind and arched his brows and smiled at her, as if to encourage her to comment on the cause of her mirth. Rosie obliged him, muttering, "I'm alive." She nodded her head and beat her thumb on her chest, as if to say, Yes, me, Rosie Campbell, alive and well and managing after all! But the stranger, who was clearly English, must have been alarmed by her gesture, for his smile disintegrated, and when Rosie laughed again, even louder than before and with tears welling up in her eyes, he snapped his newspaper up before his face and feigned immediate and thorough absorption.

THE QUEEN OF DIAMONDS

THE WIND WAS UP, AND THE DANDELION fluff that whirled through the air was as thick as snowflakes. Lina Wolff walked through it at a good clip, mumbling her prayers, and because the country road had no shoulder, simultaneously listening for cars coming from behind. Lina, who was dying, had started walking only recently, at her doctor's suggestion. The praying she had begun some time ago, when she was still well.

She was on her way back to her development, which was located in the town of Spotsdale in upstate New York. The zoning there required that the houses be at least two-thousand square feet in size and built on a minimum of two acres. Lina's house was three-thousand square feet, a cedar-sided contemporary with lots of windows, and her lot, which was on four acres, retained just enough foliage to give the illusion of rural seclusion. She and Gordon had devised the plans for both the house and the landscaping themselves. It was one of the nicest residences in Sylvan Estates.

Spotsdale itself was relatively crime free, but Sylvan Estates was an aberration in that otherwise lower- to middle-income community, and when some young miscreant did want to filch a TV or a handful of jewels, that was where he went. For this reason, Lina had several locks on all the doors, and it took her time to find the right keys and let herself in. She had stopped praying by then, and as soon as she entered the kitchen, she set about pondering the contents of the refrigerator and the topic she would bring up with Gordon once she'd eaten. Both required careful consideration. Her chemotherapy sessions were once every two weeks, and as she was midway between appointments, the nausea from the last session had all but abated and the voracity that she would experience before the next not yet begun. She decided on some cottage cheese, fresh strawberries, crackers, and tea. While she ate, she deliberated further on the other matter.

"What I could never understand about you, Gordon," she said later, as she swept the cracker crumbs from the table, "is how you could be so two-faced. For example, do you remember the last birthday gift we gave to Georgie?"

She turned to dump the crumbs into the trash can and went to the stove to heat up more water. "First of all, since Georgie is my sister's son, it would have been appropriate for me to be involved in the choosing of the gift too. But no, you had to go out and get it yourself. I should be glad, right? You saved me a trip to the mall. But Gordon, a BB gun for a four-year-old?"

She poured the water over the tea bag and returned to the table with her cup. "And when he opened it, my sister glared at us. Do you remember that? And I said, as I told you beforehand I would, 'Trish, I had nothing to do with this. Gordon took it upon himself—' And you interrupted, charmingly of course, smiling your charming smile, and gave Trish this song and dance about how kids see guns in the hands of cartoon characters on TV daily, rat-a-tat-tat, rat-a-tat-tat, and then the first time they accidentally come into contact with a real gun, they pick it up and rat-a-tat-tat, and the kid or someone else gets hurt. But now that Georgie had come by a gun by design, you could point out the safety features and how to use them, how to hold the thing and the rest of it, and that would never happen to him.

"Well, Trish bought it, didn't she?…her being a single parent and so afraid all the time that Georgie would suffer from a lack of male influence. And on and on you went, Mr. Charming, laughing when Georgie pointed the thing at us, pushing the barrel down with one hand while the other flew out to emphasize how sincere you were about coming by to teach Georgie this and that and the other thing. And then, on the way home in the car, yourself again—" She stopped to sip her tea and prod her memory, for the incident had taken place over two years ago and she wanted to be as accurate as possible in her account of it. "—you said, 'Don't you think you were giving Trish and Georgie mixed signals, letting them know that you didn't condone the choice of the gun, that I was the one who picked it out?' And I said, 'Hey, I told you beforehand that I intended to let them know that.' And you slowed down for the light and turned to me with that look on your face and said, 'Don't you ever say hey to me, woman.' And I said, 'Sorry, I forgot my place.' And you said, 'That's right, you did.' And then you wouldn't speak to me for the next several days."

Lina, who had worked herself up, stood and leaned over the table. "Do you remember that, Gordon? For two years, Gordon, two years, every time I surfaced to say something you either criticized me or spoke to me like I was a second-class citizen. And after a while I reverted into silence, because that was the only safe place for me. Two years I spent in that place, and I hated every minute of it. This is a better place now," she shouted, and she used her palm to strike the flat surface of scarred skin that covered her broken heart.

Lina had more to say, but the doorbell rang just then. She used her napkin to dab at her tears and went to answer it.

The doorbell rang often since Lina took sick. This time it was Carol, who lived in the sprawling ranch across the street. She came by frequently, leaving her husband and children to fend for themselves for an hour or so. As she had come by seldom before Lina got sick, Lina suspected that her concern was linked to Lina's wealth. People came out of the woodwork like roaches when a wealthy woman was slinking toward death. "Am I too early?" Carol asked.

"No," said Lina. "I just finished." She made an attempt to smile.

Carol, who was beaming, stepped past Lina and into the living room and stopped there for a moment to admire the mahogany shelves, the pale sofas, the peach-colored carpet, and the soft lighting that accentuated them all. Lina's therapist had said that it was time for her to begin to treat herself like a queen, and these furnishings, which were all new, were Lina's response to that. Carol had seen them before of course, but coming from a house with three children and a husband who she often referred to as a slob, she never tired of contemplating Lina's serene and tasteful existence. When she'd had her fill, she walked into the kitchen, and Lina went to put on the tea kettle once again.

"So," Carol said, sitting, "what did you and Gordon speak about tonight?"

Lina turned from the stove, indignant. "Gordon and I don't speak," she said. "I speak. Gordon either listens or doesn't, but that's beside the point."

"Sorry," Carol said, and she showed Lina her bottom lip—though Lina knew very well that she didn't bruise that easily.

Lina turned back to the stove and poured the tea in silence. She knew too that Carol repeated their conversations to Jack, her husband, when she went home. She imagined that they laughed at her, over their brandy and their pot and whatever else they consumed in preparation for their love-making, which, according to Carol, was a nightly affair. But Lina brought the tea cups over and sat down and told Carol all about the gun anyway, because her therapist, whose name was Claire Wakefield, had said that the telling of these events was the only road to catharsis, the only hope for a bit more life.

What had happened was this: One day, four years earlier, Gordon came home from a doctor's appointment beside himself because he'd learned that he had a peptic ulcer. At the time, Lina didn't see why he should be so upset. He had gone to the doctor fearing he might have something far worse. The ulcer, she thought, was good news.

But Gordon, who had never been sick a day in his life, who had never had anything happen to him of which he was not the author—Gordon, whose favorite poem was "Invictus"—simply could not deal with the fact that his condition could deteriorate at any time, that an acute perforation of the wall of his stomach might occur, or worse, the destruction of a blood vessel, which could result in a massive hemorrhaging. In short, Gordon, who had somehow gone forty-two years thinking that he could subdue Death just the way he subdued his employees at his investment firm, and his clients too when it was necessary, had had his first taste of reality.

Initially, Lina tried to soften the blow by offering him more love, but Gordon refused to accept it. In fact, he found her munificence condescending; she was minimizing his condition, he said, and in so doing, betraying him as well. Then Lina, who had been in therapy since her mother's death some years earlier, suggested that he see someone, and that was the beginning of the end.

Lina never met the woman he went to, but she felt as if she had, and she despised her. There was a reason why Gordon had an ulcer, his therapist (whose first name was Ruth and whose surname Gordon had refused to divulge) explained, and after three or four sessions, she and Gordon were able to determine what it was—or rather, who. Gordon came home from his appointments furious at Lina, at first for things that had happened years earlier. For instance, when they had first married, Lina had wanted to have children, but Gordon, who knew he would one day be a rich man, who wanted the freedom to travel, to pick up at will and do what he would, refused. Lina acquiesced, as far as she knew, for she was madly in love with him at that time and wanted only what he wanted. But the subject came up now and again over the years, and now Gordon insisted that Lina had persecuted him, had made him feel profoundly guilty for something that had been settled from the get-go. Lina considered this over and over again, but she could not see how her asking him, perhaps twice annually, whether he had changed his mind constitut-ed persecution. When she tried to explain her feelings on the matter,

Gordon told her to take her feelings to her own therapist. "This is about me!" he screamed, bobbing up and down on his toes, delivering blows to his chest with his thumb. "Me, Lina! I'm the one who's sick. I'm the one who could be dying!"

There were other things too. Lina had a habit of having a good-sized glass of wine before going to bed, and until he learned he had an ulcer, Gordon had joined her more often than not. They had discussed it many times in the past, and it was always Gordon who said that a little bit of wine was probably medicinal and nothing they should concern themselves with. But when he found out about his ulcer, he gave up the wine altogether, and as Lina had not, he reported it to Ruth. Together, Ruth and Gordon determined that Lina was an alcoholic, and that therefore Gordon must be a codependent. Ruth gave Gordon a book to read, and it explained the problem precisely: An alcoholic had deep-rooted problems; that was why she drank. And a codependent, who was generous to a fault by nature, spent his life trying to take care of these problems which were not his to begin with, and meanwhile wore himself down.

Gordon was armed then; he had created a mythology for himself. He read the book four times over, memorizing those sections that described the tolerance, the sacrifice, indeed, the self-abnegation, with which the codependent came to live. Lina, meanwhile, gave up her nightly ritual, but neither Gordon nor Ruth seemed to care. Once an alcoholic, always an alcoholic, they said. Never mind that it cost Lina no effort at all to put the bottle aside, that she found she enjoyed a glass of mineral water just as much. Her defect had already been cast in stone, as had Gordon's response to it: Gordon was a codependent. He had given away too much of himself, and now, as a result, he was sick. Enraged, he moved into the guest room and refused to have any discussions with Lina which he thought might have the potential to upset him and thereby make him sicker. Even when Lina's father, with whom she had never gotten along, died and she went to him pleading to speak about her mixed feelings, Gordon refused to hear her out.

And he began to criticize her on other matters too. She had owned a boutique for years, but when Gordon's firm began to make so much money, she'd sold it and spent her time thereafter doing volunteer work, teaching illiterate people in the community to read. She'd been using him, Gordon said. He was nothing to her but a paycheck while she herself contributed zilch to the household. She cleaned, Lina countered, she cooked, she paid the bills and kept things running generally. Wasn't that contributing to the household? No, it was not, Gordon said. They had no pets, no children; what was there to clean? And cooking, well that took a lot of effort, didn't it?

Of course Lina spoke of these matters to her own therapist, who said that it was not unusual for a controlling person like Gordon to go a bit overboard when he felt threatened, that he would come back to himself, that Lina had only to decide whether or not she wanted to wait. Lina waited. Since she was not allowed to talk to him about anything that had to do with herself, she tried to distract him from his concerns by telling him amusing anecdotes about other people, but Gordon never laughed. She tried to put her arms around him and coax him up to what had formerly been their bedroom, but he slapped her arms away and told her it was too late for that. Once, she came downstairs totally nude and stood in front of the TV, which Gordon had been watching. But Gordon only hit the on/off with the remote and went into the kitchen to stare out the window until she had gone away again. Thinking that Gordon would be happier if she gave up her volunteer work and took a job, Lina sought employment. But the economy was bad at the time, and as Lina had been out of the work force for some years, she was able to find nothing. She spoke to Gordon about opening a new boutique, but Gordon reminded her that the one she'd had years ago had never showed much of a profit, had really been for her own amusement as far as he could see, and he refused to give her the money.

One day, while he was searching for a snack in the pantry, Gordon detected a foul odor. He tore through the pantry then, frantically, and sure enough he found a bag of rotting onions way in the back, behind the boxed goods. This proved his point; not only did Lina contribute next to nothing to the household, but the little that she did do was done negligently; Lina simply didn't care.

The following day, thinking that she must appease him, if only for her own peace of mind, Lina called in sick at the Community Center where she volunteered and spent the entire day cleaning out not only the pantry but all the other cabinets and closets in the house. When she finished, she prepared a turkey breast and steamed vegetables, Gordon's dinner of choice now that he had to watch his diet, and as Gordon wasn't home yet, she sat down on the sofa with her feet up on the coffee table to rest. Unfortunately, she made the mistake of falling asleep, and Gordon came home and caught her that way. "See, this is exactly what I mean!" he shouted, and Lina was instantly transported from the arms of the mailman (whom she'd been dreaming about) to full awareness. "I work, you sleep," Gordon went on. Then he happened to come in front of her and notice that there were holes in the bottoms of her socks. "What's the matter with you?" he cried in disgust. "Don't you have any self-esteem? A grown woman with holes in her socks! This is precisely the point that's made in the book. Do you know what Ruth would say about this?"

"Gordon, I've been cleaning all day," Lina whimpered as she slid her feet from the table.

"Your day, your day!" Gordon shouted. "That's all I ever hear about is your day. I just walked in the door. Do you ask about my day? I've been working all day. Working hard, in spite of the fact that I'm a sick man who needs his rest. And all so that you can sit with your feet up on the table and snooze!"

They glared at each other then, and Lina felt a terrible hardening within herself which, although she had never experienced such a feeling before, she recognized immediately. It was a sort of inner rotation in which her natural rectitude, her integrity, swapped places with a feeling of capability such as she had never known before, the same feeling, she imagined, that had come over Lorena Bobbit just before she took up the knife. And to rid herself of it, for she knew that it was evil and would have dire consequences if she allowed it to linger, she began to pray to herself, an Our Father such as she used to say when she was a school girl.

The hardening passed, but as Lina feared its return, she continued to pray whenever Gordon scorned her, an Our Father and a Hail Mary and a Glory Be, and if he was still going on, the three of them all over again. She employed these prayers not so much in an actual attempt to speak to God as in mediation, the way a Yogi repeats a particular mantra to keep his mind emptied and oblivious to his surroundings. And it worked somewhat—not that she was actually ever able to blot out what Gordon said to her. No, she heard the words, she felt his hatred, but her own barely surfaced, and if the hardening did begin, she was able to subdue it before it overtook more rational emotions.

A habit was formed, and before long Lina prayed not only when Gordon was around and griping but whenever she was feeling blue on his account, which was most of the time. She prayed when she cleaned and she prayed when she drove to the Community Center, and she prayed when they were out with others and she was forced to watch a very different Gordon laughing and gesticulating (with more gusto than he had ever exhibited before, so that Lina knew that even then he was actually communicating with her, demonstrating for her that he had not become abominable after all, that it was only in her presence).

Lina became mischievous. Since she could no longer speak to the man about her feelings, about what she was suffering as a result of his illness (which truly didn't seem to have much of an effect on him on a day-to-day basis), she sought out other ways to take revenge. She took his boxer shorts from the hamper and used them to polish the faucets in the bathrooms. Using a tissue, she picked up the dead flies that she occasionally found on the windowsills and deposited them beneath the blankets of his bed. She found his books (he was still reading up on codependency) under the bed and moved his bookmarks forward so that he would overlook entire chapters. And each night at dinner, which was the only time they spent together anymore, generally in absolute silence, she brought the Tobasco, which she knew Gordon sorely missed, to the table and sprinkled it generously over her own plate.

In this way Lina clung to her sanity while she waited for the old Gordon, the intellectual quasi-tyrant she had married, to return to her. But in spite of all her waiting, Gordon never did return. And even after he was gone for good (it was not his peptic ulcer but an eighteen-wheeler on the freeway that got him in the end), the hard thing that was always just below the surface endured, until one day she found it with her fingers.

"Who's taking you to chemo next week?" Carol asked. "Me or Pat?"

Lina glanced up, at the calendar on the wall. "Pat," she said, observing the name scribbled on the square that marked the fifth of June.

"It's silly, you know," Carol said, "since Pat works and I don't. It doesn't make sense for her to lose the time."

"I wouldn't want to hurt her feelings," Lina mumbled. She picked up her tea cup and sipped and hoped that Carol would drop the subject. Pat lived in the development too, in one of the first homes built, and it was now shabby by comparison. Her husband's business had gone under recently, and Lina knew very well that they were struggling, for Pat didn't make any secret of it. Of course it was silly for Pat, who was temporarily the sole support of their household, to take off time from her job (she was a dental hygienist) to drive Lina to chemotherapy, but Lina figured that Pat saw it as an investment. Both women were investing time in Lina, competing with each other really. And as their competition benefited Lina—for she needed not only a ride to chemo (because she was too sick afterward to drive herself home), but also, sometimes, desperately, company—she remembered, when she was with one or both of them, to say things that suggested that Pat and Carol might benefit as result of their investments.

"I went to see my lawyer again today," Lina lied. "We've nearly got everything settled. I want everything to be in order when the time comes. I want everything to be clear."

Carol put her cup down hard. "Oh, Lina, don't talk like that. You've got to have hope. You know, you look good. Your color is good. The doctor seems to be satisfied that the chemo is working. All you need to do is believe that yourself. Mind over matter. I know you can lick this thing."

Lina stared at her, for she thought she detected some sincerity in her little speech, that maybe Carol's friendship had nothing to do with her money after all. She decided to test her further. "I'm thinking of remodeling the kitchen," she said.

Carol looked stunned. "Why? What's wrong with the way it is?"

Lina got up and got the magazine that had been on the counter with the mail. She opened it to the page with the Kitchen Exquisite ad and handed it to Carol. It depicted a huge L-shaped length of cabinets, white with black granite counters, and two free standing butcher block tables in the open area. Instead of upper cabinets, there were shelves, revealing rows of cookbooks, copper pots and pans dangling from hooks, and of course the dishes and cups, all white and in tidy rows. Above the shelves were brass-rimmed light fixtures at three-foot intervals. The range was industrial, with utensils hanging prettily all around the hood's circumference. Carol read the fine print aloud and learned that the side of the room which was not in evidence featured a pantry, spice closet, broom closet, wine vault, ironing board, and trash-compactor, all concealed behind doors and more cabinets.

"Why, this will cost a fortune!" Carol cried.

"Thirty-five thousand dollars," Lina said flatly. "I've already had someone out for an estimate. Don't you like it?"

Carol looked up at her quizzically. "Of course I like it. What's not to like? It's just that there's nothing wrong with your kitchen the way it is."

"I like this one better," Lina said, and she folded her hands on the table and smiled with resolution.

Carol blinked at her. Then she shook her head as if, Lina thought, to dispel an unseemly thought. "Well, then of course you should go ahead and do it," she said. "God only knows, if I had the money, I would. I just hope you've considered the time that it will take, the workmen that will be coming in and out, hammering, sawing, asking you for cups of coffee, glasses of water, tracking sawdust and wood chips all over your new carpeting when they need to use the bathroom…"

Carol trailed off then, for Lina was smiling full out now, with her teeth showing like they used to back in the old days before the onset of Gordon's peptic ulcer and its corollary, his lunacy. "Oh, I see," she said, and she smiled herself. "I see what you're up to."

It was no secret that in spite of everything, Lina still hoped to meet a man. She had grieved deeply after Gordon's accident, not for the Gordon with the peptic ulcer but for the one she remembered from before that, the one who, notwithstanding his authoritative ways, had often been loving at least. And then, when she first found the lump, she began to grieve for the monster himself, because if his treatment of her could result in such a thing (and she believed that was the case), then it was entirely possible that her treatment of him could have produced the ulcer, though what she had done wrong exactly she still couldn't say. Claire Wakefield had worked hard to get her to dismiss this notion (Lina's after-dinner confrontations with

Gordon's phantom, her stating now all the things that she had not been allowed to say before, were a part of the process), but she was never quite successful. In any case, between Lina's two-year-long imposed silence with Gordon, and then the grieving period thereafter, Lina became recklessly withdrawn. Then one night she happened to rent a movie about a naturally passionate woman who, as a result of a series of injustices, had become reclusive, and Lina awakened to the fact that she had once been passionate too. And in the days that followed she began to feel such a hunger for her passionate self that she thought that might kill her before the other. That was when she decided she must have the love of a man.

She turned to God at first, whose evocation, though it had not kept her animosity from manifesting itself physically, had at least kept her from murdering Gordon. She prayed more directly, beginning with an Our Father just to get His attention, and then, when she felt she had got it, speaking to Him outright, casually, in much the same tone that she spoke to Claire Wakefield. "I need someone to love me, someone whom I can love," she said, aloud if she were home and in her head if she were out walking. "It doesn't matter what he looks like, just someone who's kind, someone who will care about how I feel and who will want to be with me when the time comes for me to leave this world."

Did God answer? It's hard to say. Lina wasn't beautiful, but certainly she was attractive, and men had always been drawn to her. And she was petite and sweet-faced, so that when her wit, which could be sharp, surfaced, it was always a surprise. Her laughter was raspy rather than melodious, and it seemed too large for a woman her size, but then that was one of her charms. She had no useful knowledge (it was her computer illiteracy which had kept her from finding a job), but she had studied literature and mythology and philosophy in college, and there were many subjects she could talk about.

Her chemotherapy sessions kept her from going out as much as she would have liked, and on the nights when she had to contend with the nausea, she stayed at home and read. But as soon as she felt herself again, she was out and about, with friends when she could manage it and alone when she could not.

There was, for instance, a New Age bookstore in Spotsdale where various authors came to give workshops and promote their books. More women attended than men, but as the subject matter was always healing of one sort of another, Lina assumed that the men who did attend would be more or less sensitive types. At a lecture on the healing powers of sound one night she found herself sitting next to a tall lanky man with tousled gray hair and a wild look in his eye. Fred Feat, the guest author for that evening, taught the assemblage to emit a humming sound from their throats and to concentrate on the effect, the gentle vibration that the humming produced in their bodies as well as their minds. While they hummed (on and on—they were told not stop), Fred Feat spoke in a trance-like voice about the mending they were undergoing. And since Lina of all people could certainly do with some mending, she tried her best to follow his discourse. But she fell short, because her mind kept straying to the wild-eyed man beside her. She suspected that he was an intellectual, perhaps a writer too, perhaps a poet. She suspected that his wild look was a result of too much acid taken back in the sixties, in his quest to learn as much about himself and the world as possible. She envisioned a life for him, reading his poetry to enthralled audiences in dark cafes by night and selling vacuum cleaners by day in order to put bread on the table. He was the kind of man, she decided, who had suffered so many emotional lacerations in his life that he would view her disfigurement as a link between them, a symbol of their combined sufferings, and cherish her all the more for it.

By the time they stopped humming and were taking turns expounding on the benefits the session had produced for them individually, Lina was already wondering whether or not she had made the bed that morning. "I feel," said the wild-eyed man when his turn came, "I feel…" and as if he were calculating the amount of humidity in the air rather than his sentiments, he turned his palms upward and tilted his head toward the ceiling. Those in the front rows, meanwhile, turned around to see what was detaining him. "I feel like a refrigerator," he said at last.

Lina was the first to laugh, and because her laughter was contagious, everyone else followed suit. "No, really, I feel good," the wild-eyed man, whose face had reddened, said when the laughter subsided.

"Good," said Fred Feat, and then he and the others looked to Lina.

Lina, who wanted the wild-eyed man to know something about her, said, "I feel very relaxed. I feel the way I do when I listen to classical music at home. I live alone, so it's always quiet in my house, but it's only when I'm listening to music that I'm actually able to lose myself. And now I've found an alternative method, something I can do when I'm driving or out taking a walk."

Fred Feat nodded; this was the kind of thing he liked to hear. Lina, who was happy to have pleased him, smiled at him and then turned her smile on the wild-eyed man, who smiled back at her. Later, as they were filing out of the bookstore, Lina turned to the wild-eyed man again, and, extending her hand, introduced herself. "Milton Fleet," he responded. "So what are you, divorced?"

"No," Lina said, "Widowed. What about you?"

"Divorced," he said. "Ten years now."

They crossed the street and headed toward the municipal parking lot. The night was cool and full of stars. "There's this little game I play," Lina said. "When I'm in a room with people I don't know, I try to guess things about them. I figure you for a poet...or a writer of some sort."

Milton laughed. "Not even close."

Lina tried again. "Lit professor?"

"No. Give up?"

"This is my car," Lina said, and she stopped beside her baby blue Cadillac and put her finger to her lips. "I don't know," she said. "I do give up. Tell me."

"Electrolux."

Lina could only stare.

"I'm one of the top salesmen in the district. I've got a company car," he said, and he pointed to the Toyota two spaces down. "What about you?"

"Volunteer work," Lina answered, although she'd quit that back when she'd had the mastectomy.

"No, I mean, what kind of vacuum cleaner do you use? I've got one of ours in the trunk. I could show you."

"No thanks," Lina said.

"Come on. You live nearby? I could give you a demonstration right now. No obligation or anything like that. What do you say?"

Lina stepped closer to him. "Listen, Milt. Let me ask you something. What did you really think of the session tonight?"

"You mean really?"

"Your gut reaction."

Milton Fleet shook his head. "I hate shit like that. I hate the kind of stuff everyone was saying afterward, 'I feel this' and 'I feel that.' Tell you the truth, I feel like an ass for having sat through it."

"I could tell you why that is," Lina mumbled, but Fred didn't hear her.

"We get a bonus at the end of the year," he explained, "depending on how much we sell. And how much we sell depends on our confidence level, ultimately. And of course our ability to persuade. That's what I came looking for. When I heard 'sound therapy,' I figured it meant the sound of your voice, something of that nature, how to project yourself so as to get people to listen. I sure as hell didn't think we were going to have to sit there like a fu…like a damn refrigerator and…Hey, where you going?"

"Home," Lina said, and she unlocked her car door.

And so it went. Wherever she went, she managed to meet a man, but not one of the men she met turned out to be Mr. Right. At a bar in Riverview, where she had gone with Iris, a divorcee who was only too happy to have someone to gallivant with, she talked to a man all evening who admitted, at the end of the night, to being married and then asked Lina if she would take him home with her anyway. ("Why didn't you?" Iris asked later. "He was cute; I would have. A one night stand is better than none at all.")

After that, Lina asked the men she met about their marital status right from the start. And while a good many confessed that they were in fact married, an equal number hesitated just long enough before saying they weren't so that Lina knew they were lying and bade them farewell as quickly as the others. And of the single ones, there seemed to be two types. There were those whose eyes brightened when they learned that Lina lived in Sylvan Estates, so that Lina felt certain that they were more interested in her assets than in her character, and there were those who appeared to be just about perfect until Lina confided that she'd had a mastectomy and saw their smiles freeze on their faces.

She talked to Pat about it one night. They were out at a French restaurant, and although Lina suspected that Pat would never have agreed to come if Lina hadn't finally said, "Come on, it will be my treat," Pat's response to Lina's dilemma was, "The worst is the money thing. That someone would actually come out and ask you what you're worth…My God! That's just incredible to me."

They were speaking specifically of the last man Lina had met. He had pulled up at the Parents Without Partners dance (which Lina figured she was entitled to attend since she had always wanted to be a parent) at the same time as Lina, and the first thing he said to her was, "Hey, nice car!" Lina should have known then, but as he didn't bring up the subject of her Cadillac all the time they were dancing, she let herself forget about that. He was an artist, a painter, and after a brief exchange of their personal histories, he spoke to her about the various projects he was currently involved in, the shows he'd had in the past and the ones he anticipated having in the future. Lina listened attentively, and so passionately did he speak of his artistic life that she became increasingly certain that he was the one and was just getting up the nerve to mention her mastectomy when he said, "I could use a sponsor, just until my next showing. What do you say? Do you think you could swing it? You must have gotten some kind of a settlement after your husband's accident."

"It's the way of the world now," Lina said to Pat. She had ordered only a salad but was vicariously enjoying the creamed cod that Pat was devouring. "I don't know what happened to the Age of Aquarius and all that business. You know, I was driving down the road the other day, and I turned on one of those stations that the twelve-year-olds listen to? I was feeling really low and I was thinking about the kind of stuff we used to hear on the radio when we were kids...you know, *Why Must I Be a Teenager in Love*...that sort of thing? I mean, I'm not stupid. I know about heavy metal and rap and all that, but I thought, if I could just hear one song about love sickness, one little ditty that would prove that love is still something to strive for somewhere..."

Pat sat forward with her elbows on the table. She was a big woman with a horsy face, and every time she moved, the table shook. Lina couldn't imagine her bending over her patients, lowering sharp instruments into their mouths. "Here's what I think, Lina," she said. "You can't do much about the ones who are appalled by your single-breastedness," (Lina cringed, as she always did when Pat put it that way) "but you can do something about the money-mongers. I mean look at you! You look like a wealthy woman!"

Lina lifted her brows. "That's what I am, Pat."

"Lina, hear me out. You arrive at these places that you go to in your fancy car with all your gold jewelry gleaming and your expensive clothes, and then you're surprised when the ones you attract happen to be looking for a well-to-do. Sell the Cadillac. Or put it in the garage and get yourself some old junker to drive when you're on the prowl." (Lina cringed again.) "And start buying your clothes at K-Mart. And as for the jewelry, put it in your safe deposit box and I'll give you some of mine to wear. Then at least we can eliminate the money-mongers from the scene. Have no doubt about it."

Lina laughed at the time, but she got to thinking about it and decided it might not be such a bad idea. Her house had been full of men of late (the renovations on her kitchen were in progress) and there was not one of them who had not mentioned how fortunate she was to be able to afford such an extravagance—though none had put it quite that way. And as they didn't realize that she was merely satisfying whims that would soon be put to rest along with her ailing body, the carpenters pressed her to let them add on a nice deck in the back, or better yet a sun room, and the painter, who should have known just by looking that the rest of the house had only recently been painted, urged her to consider a change of colors.

She ignored them all after the first few days, and until the kitchen was completed, she was sorry she had ever agreed to have the job done in the first place. She was out of her mind, she decided. She had been a gourmet cook once, but that was back before Gordon's ulcer. And then afterward, when Claire Wakefield had finally managed to convince her that it was perfectly all right for her to dine on gourmet fare herself, the other problem had come up, and the dinners that she had so enjoyed creating were no longer consistently palatable. Now she hardly cooked at all, and when she dined out, she stuck to salads or entrees that had no creams or sauces. And here she had a kitchen that Craig Claiborne would have envied. For what? she asked herself.

But the truth of the matter was that when the carpenters and the painter and the mason left and Lina found herself alone with her latest impulse, she was happy (briefly, at least) and she invited both Pat and Carol over to come and see.

"What I would do for a house like this one. Why, with the paint peeling off my own house and no money coming in to do anything about it…This place is a palace, Lina," Pat said, and the look Carol gave her just then assured Lina that Carol was thinking that Pat had gone too far in hinting that the house might be up for grabs along with Lina's money.

Actually, it was all up for grabs at this point, for Lina had not even been to see a lawyer yet. She had no idea to whom she should leave the greater part of her assets. Her sister and Georgie, of course, would inherit some, but Trish, who worked for Merrill Lynch, had made a killing in the stock market back in the early eighties when everyone else was expecting a radical decline and selling out, and she could live on the interest her investments generated alone if she chose to. And furthermore, Lina had gone to her once to ask to borrow a few thousand dollars so that she could buy Gordon, who had always wanted to learn to sail, a week on the Chesapeake for his birthday, and Trish had refused. "You've got plenty of money," she'd said. "Just take it out of the checking." Lina had tried to explain that it wouldn't be the same, paying for Gordon's gift with Gordon's money, that she would take on some odd job and pay her back in no time, but Trish had remained unbending, and Lina had never forgotten that. So now, on top of the nausea, the prospect of her life being taken from her shortly, on top of the fact that she couldn't find a decent man, and the even more disturbing fact that for all that she longed for His voice, for all that she spoke to Him a good part of every day, He didn't seem moved to speak to her, she had this other matter to consider.

It was too much at times, and although she tried her damnedest to keep her spirits high, there were entire days where she was unable to distract herself from her self-pity. She stayed in bed and cried then, and when she was not talking to God, she talked to herself, repeating the recommendations that Claire Wakefield had made about her taking care of herself, doing special things for herself, permitting herself to act on her impulse, and so on. She longed to return to the routine of her volunteer work, but between the doctors' appointments, the chemotherapy and the bad days that followed it, and the sessions with Claire, any semblance of routine was out of the question. She was fine when she had a good book to read, but so many of the books that she came home with turned out to be, in spite of their literary pretensions, well-written romances that ended when love began, with the protagonist and his or her significant other walking off into a figurative sunset that Lina knew didn't exist.

One night she was invited to Carol's house for dinner, for some Chinese concoction to which Carol promised not to add any MSG. Lina declined at first, for health reasons. Carol was none too clean to begin with, and between the dog hair and the snotty-nosed children, Lina feared that she would pick up some germ there, which, of course, would only hasten the defeat of her already overworked white blood cells. Lina, who wasn't shy, explained all this to Carol, but Carol swore that she had just completed her spring cleaning and that the kids were as healthy as the rose bushes that were now in bloom in Lina's garden. Earlier that same week, Pat, whose husband had still not found a job and who was now claiming to be destitute, had come to Lina's house with a gift, a pair of earrings that Lina suspected Pat had received as a gift herself and, in spite of her bad taste, had found too gaudy to wear. But the wrapping paper had been tasteful at least, and Lina, who was on the giving end of gift-giving far more often than on the receiving, had exclaimed. Now she imagined that Pat had bragged to Carol about her meager offering, and that Carol's dinner invitation was merely an effort not to be outdone. In Lina's mind, her acceptance of the invitation would very likely provoke Pat to some greater kindness yet, which in turn would compel Carol to attempt to surpass her again. And thus Lina agreed to take the risk.

The dinner itself was boring. For all that Carol claimed that Jack was something of a wizard when it came to their intimate relations, his talent for stimulating dinner conversation was near to non-existent. He owned a factory which manufactured, among other things, ant farms, and except for when he had to stop talking to tell the children, who were constantly interrupting, to "clam up," he spoke exclusively of the exploits of the revolting creatures—and this in spite of the fact that there were a good many unrecognizable dark things in Carol's concoction. By the time they had finished their entrees and the children had left the table in search of more hospitable surroundings, Lina knew far more than she had ever wished to know about ants. "They talk to each other," Jack disclosed, his hands spread apart, his head twitching with amazement. "When one wants to get the attention of the other, she taps him on the head with her feelers."

Lina turned her blank look on Carol, whose grin revealed that she thought the world of Jack—or maybe of the talking ants. "She?" Lina asked, turning back to Jack. "Are they all females then that you supply for these kits that you make?"

"Precisely," Jack said. "The male ants, the princes, mate with the queen and then die immediately thereafter. The ones we supply for the kits, the workers, are all female. There's no point in supplying males. Or queens either, for that matter."

"How interesting," Lina said, and she turned to Carol again. "Do you mind if I go see what the kids are up to?"

She found the two younger ones, Sissy and Gloria, sprawled on the sofa in the living room in front of the television. They were watching a sitcom, grunting in unison with the canned laughter, though Lina suspected the jokes went over their heads. Gloria, the six-year-old, scratched a lot, Lina had noticed, and she was scratching now, under her armpit first, and then along her neck. Gloria, who was two years younger, was using her index finger to trace the circumference of her right nostril. Lina decided against conversing with either of them and went off to find Jack Junior, or J.J., as he was called.

She found him in his room, where he was so intent on the Nintendo game that he was playing that he didn't hear her come in. Finally she cleared her throat, startling J.J., who consequently failed to make the little man on the screen jump in time to avoid the monster that was pursuing him. "Damn!" J.J. cried, and then, when he turned and saw that it was Lina, "Sorry."

J.J. returned to his game, and Lina, who had never come into contact with Nintendo before, sat down on the edge of his unmade bed to watch. When he saw that she was interested, he began to explain the objective to her in a pretentious tone not unlike the one his father had used in his insect discourse. The little men, he said, were the Super Mario Brothers, and there were eight worlds which they had to go through, each of which had four levels, before they could get to the princess, who had to be saved. There were treasures to be found along the way, coins to be collected, and mushrooms and flowers that, once ingested, provided the little men with more mass and ammunition respectively. There were also monsters of various dispositions to contend with. "Just like real life," Lina commented, and J.J. shot her a glance.

Carol came to the door. Dessert was on the table, she said, and as she and Lina went down the hall in pursuit of it, she confided that ever since J.J. had got the thing, he had become tense and irritable and so intent on beating the games that he played that he often refused to go out and play with his friends the way a healthy twelve-year-old should.

"It's really that bad?" Lina asked.

"You watch," Carol said. "He won't even come in for dessert now that he's gotten started. And when I go in to kiss him goodnight, he'll yell at me and tell me I just caused the death of one of his men. I'm telling you, there's something evil about the damn thing, about the way it holds his attention. He simply can't be distracted from it."

"That's awful," Lina said, and she determined then and there that she would go to the toy store in the morning and buy one for herself.

Lina set up the Nintendo in the living room and J.J. came over to start her off. She had bought several other games besides Super Mario Brothers, but she found herself so uncoordinated that she soon agreed to let J.J. borrow them until she got the first one down. It took her an entire day to get to the end of the first level of the first world, and even though she died immediately upon her arrival in the second level, she was thrilled with her progress and telephoned J.J. to let him know. Carol answered, and as there was more than a trace of resentment in her tone, Lina knew that she wasn't happy about the additional games that had come into the house.

"Anything wrong?" Lina asked.

"Well, Lina…" Carol began.

But Lina cut her off saying, "I really need to speak to J.J. quickly because I'm waiting for a call. I gave my lawyer a list last week? A who-gets-which-piece-of-jewelry? And he's having his secretary call me back to confirm everything before it gets typed and added to the other documents."

Carol was silent for a moment. Then, without bothering to cover the phone, she yelled, "J.J. It's Aunt Lina…and don't forget to thank her for all the games she loaned you!" and to Lina, "You're so good with the kids. You made J.J.'s day. Oh, here he is now. You take care of your business and I'll speak to you later."

Lina continued to be so enthralled with the game in the days that followed that she had to set the timer on her new stove so that she would remember to stop and eat. And then she was in such a hurry to get back to it again that she put in almost no time considering her daily confrontations with Gordon, and consequently her harangues were not nearly as forceful as they once had been. One night, in fact, she had completed her entire dinner before she realized that she hadn't given Gordon a single thought. "Listen up, Gordon," she said when she finally remembered him. "I can't really talk to you tonight. I haven't prepared. And I've got this game in there." And as if he were actually sitting there at the table, watching her with his inscrutable owl eyes, she pointed towards the living room. Then all at once she sighed and folded her hands on the table. "Gordon, do you remember when we first started going out? How enthusiastic we both were then?" She blinked back tears that had arisen out of nowhere. "Remember that time up in Maine? How it rained all the way up? And how we were disgusted and thought we'd have to spend the entire weekend indoors? And then we stopped at that little restaurant on the coast—and it was so foggy and rainy that we couldn't even see the ocean? Remember the lobsters we had? How the juices ran down our arms? How we laughed at each other? And the next thing we knew the rain had stopped? And then the fog lifted? And we saw not only the ocean but all the little islands that dotted it? And we ran out into the sunshine and took off our shoes and walked in a few feet of icy cold water to the nearest of the islands and sat for so long talking about how unexpected they had been? About unexpected things generally? And then the tide came in and we had to swim back? And it was so cold and we couldn't stop laughing?

"Oh, Gordon, we didn't know what unexpected was then, did we? Islands in the sea emerging from the fog, we thought it was. We never planned on hell on earth."

She stood up slowly. "I did love you once, Gordon. I want you to know that. You were the one true love of my life," she whispered, and on her way to the living room, she stopped once to look over her shoulder and smile at him.

Had Lina been a better player, she might have gone on playing right up until the end, but as it turned out, she never got past the fourth world, and after a few weeks she became frustrated and disconnected the thing. Still, a few weeks of distraction from her problems was no small thing, and thinking that she might go on in that vein, she bought crossword puzzle books, jigsaw puzzles, and a new deck of cards for Solitaire. But none of these did the trick, and before very long she was praying again. "Okay, God," she said one afternoon after she had gotten off the phone with Iris, with whom she would be going out that evening. She'd been sitting on the edge of her bed, but as she was particularly determined to have His ear, she slipped down to the carpet to kneel with her hands folded and pointed in His direction. "Maybe I've been asking for too much," she went on, "by asking for someone whom I can love. I don't know…maybe I'm picky. Or maybe, after everything that happened with Gordon, I'm simply not capable of loving anyone anymore. Just let me find someone who can love me. That's all I ask. And let it be tonight, if You don't mind, because to tell You the truth, I haven't been feeling well at all the last few weeks, and I don't know how much longer I've got."

Having finished her prayer, Lina got off her knees. But she found that she felt light-headed, and she took this to mean that maybe God was finally listening now that she had tempered her request (indeed, maybe He was considering granting it), and so she continued talking to Him on and off for the rest of the afternoon.

She was flipping through a men's fashion supplement that had come with the *Times* when it occurred to her that it would be really helpful if He would give her some indication as to what the man who could love her might be wearing when she saw him, hopefully later that night. "If only You would speak to me outright just once, just one word," she pleaded. "If You would only say 'Green,' or 'Stripes,' or 'Short Sleeves'—anything that would help narrow it down."

She had an idea then. She jumped up from the table, flew into her bedroom, and returned to the kitchen a moment later with a small fan, which she quickly set up on the table. Then she positioned the magazine so that when she turned the fan on, the pages would flutter. "I'll close my eyes and count to three," she told God. "And then I'll turn off the fan, and whatever page the magazine has opened to, whatever page You make it open to, I'll assume that my man will be wearing pretty much the same thing as that man on that page, because of course I wouldn't expect anyone who could love me to actually look like any of the models." She rubbed her forehead with her palm, and recalling that it was those who actually believed that their prayers would be answered who in fact had them answered, she revised her petition. "I will know," she said emphatically, and she added, just for good measure, "I really appreciate this, Father...Dad."

She waited a moment, long enough, she hoped, for God to acquiesce, and then she took a deep breath, placed her finger on the toggle switch, closed her eyes, turned on the fan, and counted. At three, she turned it off again and reached for the magazine, which had indeed blown open. But when she opened her eyes, the man she found herself looking at (and he had to be the one because the page across from him was all print) wasn't wearing anything!

The ad was for a cologne called Sundown, and in the right-hand corner there was a picture of the bottle itself. The man, who was lying in the surf of some body of water or another, was depicted from the chest up, with his head turned aside so that only the shape of his cheekbone was discernible. The water he lay in glittered with moonlight, as did the droplets that had accumulated on his skin. There were so many shadows on his chest, for of course the photo was supposed to make one think of dusk, that Lina couldn't even tell whether it was hairy or not.

Lina was beside herself. Was this God's idea of a joke? She flipped through the remaining pages, all of which revealed men in a good light and fully dressed. She was tempted to scream at God, the way she screamed at Gordon's phantom, but then she remembered that He responded to the faithful, and she came to think that this might be a test of her faith. She turned back to the Sundown ad and scrutinized it again for some clue that she had neglected the first time around. "Sundown," she mumbled, "Sundown." She lifted her gaze to look at her bag and car keys, still on the counter where she had left them when she'd come home from picking up the *Times* and her bagel that morning. It was late in the afternoon, but she thought the Spotsdale pharmacy might still be open.

Iris had been, to use Pat's phrase, "on the prowl" for years, and because Lina suspected that she would go just about anywhere if she thought she might find a man there, Lina had always dictated their destination when the two went out together. But on this occasion, Lina was disinclined to do so. She was leaving things in His hands, and if that meant trusting Him to have some sway over Iris, well then, so be it. "You really don't care?" Iris asked at a red light, her heavily made-up face inclined toward Lina's.

The two women were not friends. They had met at a party the year before and through their conversation had ascertained that they had the one thing, their interest in the opposite sex, in common. Except for the obvious differences (Iris wore cheap, tight, low-cut dresses, push-up bras, and her bleached hair teased) the two knew virtually nothing about each other. But as neither had other single friends to go out with, they'd exchanged phone numbers. "That's right," Lina said. She was sitting stiffly in the passenger seat with her eyes straight ahead and her hands folded on her Gucci bag. "You go ahead and decide tonight."

Iris pressed her lips together pensively. "I've got it then! Harold's Gum House. How's that sound?"

Lina stiffened further, but in the end she managed an assenting nod.

Harold's Gum House, it turned out, was a country western bar about forty miles north of Spotsdale, in the town of Bearsdon. As soon as they pulled up in front of it, a dingy, flat-roofed building in a wooded setting, Lina knew it was not her kind of place. The windows were opened, which of course meant that there was no air-conditioning to offset the heat and humidity. And the noise that came wafting out, a kind of mass howling with some jukebox music in the background, indicated that the crowd would be rowdy.

In fact, it was so crowded they had to turn sideways to get through the door. To the right was the bar itself, though Lina couldn't actually see it with all the people pressed around. To the left were several tables, very close together, and beyond them the dance floor, and those who were on it danced wildly, with the clumsy gestures of drunks. Lina, who liked quiet places with jazzy music, decided that she had gone too far by letting Iris take the reins like that. And she was about to tell her so when she noticed Iris's smile and the gleam that came to her eyes as she turned her head to take in the assemblage. Clearly, Iris was in her element here, and thinking that if Iris at least met a man, the evening wouldn't be a total waste, Lina restrained herself once more. "I'll be right back," she shouted into Iris's ear, and she made her way through the bedlam towards the corner which seemed most likely to contain the rest rooms—or, as was the case here, the rooms designated for Bulls and Cows.

In spite of the nature of the place, Lina decided to stick to her plan. When she'd left Iris, the band had been setting up, and one of its members, she couldn't help noticing, was very attractive. She had seen his face for only an instant, when he'd set down the amp he'd been carrying, but Lina thought he looked somewhat disgusted, and she took this to mean that he had no more liking for the place than she did.

She locked herself in a stall, opened her bag, unscrewed the cap on her bottle of Sundown, and inhaled. The scent was subtle, and as she didn't know whether she would be able to recognize it on someone with all the smoke out there, she decided to approach the handsome man from the band right away, while the scent was still fresh in her mind. As she was leaving the rest room, Lina saw that Iris had wasted no time; she was sitting at a table with three men, talking, and the men, who were leaning in to hear her, were laughing heartily. Then Iris happened to notice Lina too, and she raised her arm into the air and wiggled her fingers. Accordingly, the men all turned their heads to see who she was waving at.

Lina didn't like the looks of this trio one bit. The man on Iris's right was extremely thin and round-shouldered. His face was long and his cheeks were hollow and his eyes were slits. His wavy hair was greasy looking, and he observed Lina's approach suspiciously, as did the one on Iris's left. This one had dark rings under his eyes, and his skin had that puffy look that most people wake up with and then lose after a few cups of coffee and a hot shower. The man across from Iris was the only one of the three who was smiling—moronically, as it happened—so that Lina guessed he was drunk.

Holding up a finger to indicate that she would join them soon enough, Lina bypassed the table and made her way to the stage. The band had completed their set up, and the singer was tapping the mike with his index finger in an effort to alert the clamorous crowd to their presence. Lina, who didn't know the names of any country western songs, leaned in over the stage and motioned for the bass player, the handsome one, to approach. He got up from his stool with a half-smile and bent over so that Lina was able to put her mouth to his ear. "Do you take requests?" she asked.

He nodded and slipped a hand around to the small of his back, so that Lina knew he was uncomfortable in that position.

"Can you play *Going Home by Way of the River*?"

He shook his head. "Sorry, ma'am. Don't know that one," he said, and as he was straightening, Lina inhaled deeply, but the only thing she smelled was sweat.

Dispirited, Lina went to the table and sat in the empty seat between the drunk and the thin man. "These are Pete and Fred and Harry," Iris announced cheerfully, "and guys, this is Lina." Pete and Fred nodded. Harry, the drunk, said "Howdy do," and elbowed Lina so sharply she nearly fell off the chair. Outraged, she turned to give him a look, but his expression did not change at all. The waitress came by, and Lina ordered a Coke, which set the men to chuckling. "Big drinker," Harry said.

The band started up then, and the thin man popped up from his seat immediately, revealing himself to be well over six feet tall, and bent over to ask Iris to dance. She rose beaming, and apparently oblivious to the message that Lina was trying to communicate to her, for when their eyes met, Iris only winked. Then the next thing Lina knew, Harry was pulling her to her feet and dragging her to the dance floor too, and this in spite of her protestations.

The number was a slow one, but Harry's considerable paunch negated the possibility of them dancing too closely. As he twirled her around, humming out of tune, Lina noticed that his blotchy-faced friend was leaving the table and heading for the bar with his head hanging. "You come here often?" Harry asked.

"No," Lina said curtly, and they finished the dance in silence.

Although Harry had proven himself to be an adequate dancer for such a big man, Lina refused to let herself be pulled up from the table again. Iris and Fred had still not quit the dance floor from the last number, and Lina was hoping that Harry would go off to seek another partner and that she would be left alone to brood over the fact that she'd allowed herself to be brought here in the first place. But Harry only said that he didn't mind not dancing, that he was just as happy to talk if that was what Lina wanted, and Lina conceded that she was stuck with him for the rest of the evening and had better make the best of it. Her mood, however, soured more by the moment, and when he complimented her on her swell-looking jewelry, she replied tartly, "I'm rich," and realized that she wasn't up to the challenge after all.

Harry looked at her blankly. Then he glanced towards the dance floor. "You dance nice," he said, smiling. "How come you don't want to?"

"I'm sick," Lina snapped. "I get tired out easily. I have cancer."

"Cancer of what?" Harry asked, still smiling.

"The breast."

But the band had picked up its pace, and Harry, who hadn't heard her, put a hand aside his mouth and cried, "The what?"

"The breast," Lina shouted back at him. "My left breast is gone."

Harry looked down, at her blouse. "What'd they do, give you a phony one?"

"Yes, a prosthesis."

"A pro what?"

"A phony one," Lina hissed.

He shook his head. "Makes you wonder," he said.

"Makes you wonder what?"

He cocked his head from side to side. "Why something like that would happen to someone like you."

"I guess it's like Leonard Cohen said," Lina answered irritably.

"You know, about how when Jesus knew for certain that only drowning men could see Him?"

Harry stared at her. "Who's Lawrence Cohen?"

"Leonard," she huffed. The music was getting louder. She glanced over her shoulder and noted that the folks on the dance floor were hustling about, forming a line. She grabbed Harry's sleeve and shouted into his ear, "Suzanne takes you down to her place near the river?"

She released him, grateful a hundred times over that he smelled only of garlic and alcohol and not a trace of cologne of any sort. Then all at once she noticed that tears were clouding up his eyes. "What?" she cried.

Harry shrugged. "Suzanne," he said.

"The poem?"

"My wife."

Lina brightened. "You're married then?"

"Was. She's dead." He looked down, then over at the dancers, then back at Lina again. "You still tired out?" he asked.

"Yes," Lina lied, but he bent his head and looked so dejected just then that Lina had a change of heart. Taking his hand, she led him back out to the dance floor.

And so the evening went. Lina and Harry danced a while and returned to the table when Fred and Iris did. Afterward, a lengthy conversation about raising pigs ensued. Lina took no part in it. The men drank quite a bit more, and Iris pretty much kept up with them. At one point Lina interrupted the conversation, which had now passed on to good names for hunting dogs, to inform Iris that she, Lina, would be driving home. Iris shrugged, and when the waitress came by again, she ordered another drink.

Soon all three were quite drunk, and their words were so slurred that Lina wasn't able to follow their conversation at all. Strangely enough, they seemed to understand one another well enough, and there was much laughter among them. Every time Harry laughed, he looked at Lina, with some longing in his eye, as if to invite her to join in. But Lina had had enough by now, and it was all she could do to keep a feeble smile in place on her lips. Finally she interrupted again and told Iris that it was time to get going.

"The night's still a pup!" Iris declared, but then she began to pout and Lina knew that she had won. When she suggested that Iris use the bathroom before they got underway, Iris rose obediently, and holding on to the backs of chairs for support, made her way between the tables. When the chairs ran out, she extended her arms like a sleepwalker and wobbled forward until she finally reached her destination.

Relieved that Iris had made it without incident, Lina turned to see how the other two were doing. Fred was smiling, at nothing in particular. His hands were folded on the table, and he was twirling his long, thin thumbs. As for Harry, he was sitting stiffly, holding on to his drink with one hand and clutching the edge of the table with the other. His eyes were large and round. He looked like he'd just had a frightening thought, as if he'd just remembered that he'd left something cooking on the stove at home.

"Harry," she said, reaching for her bag, "it was nice meeting you, Harry. Maybe I'll see you again here sometime if Iris and I ever get out this way. Now you take care of yourself." She saw that Iris was returning and rose from her seat.

But Harry apparently wanted to stop her because he let go of the table edge just then and made an attempt to reach for her hand. And the next thing Lina knew, there was a thump and he was down on the floor and people from the tables nearby were twisting around in their seats to see what had happened.

His drink had gone down with him, though, miraculously, the glass hadn't broken. Lina couldn't see his face—he was all in shadows, and his head was turned aside, so that only the shape of his cheekbone was discernible—but she didn't think he was hurt. What she could see was that the puddle of whiskey he lay in glittered with reflections from the hanging lights at the bar, as did the droplets that had splattered on his face and neck.

Harry got her number from Fred (who got it from Iris) and called the very next evening. He was sorry to have passed out, he said, and he wanted the chance to make it up to her. Would she consider driving down to Harold's Gum House that night?

"Certainly not," Lina answered. God or no God, she was not about to drive forty miles by herself to watch him get drunk again. But two days passed before she heard from him again, and in that time she did a lot of thinking, and when he called again, she forced herself to mumble the words that translated to an invitation to her house the following evening for dinner.

"That'd be a tough one," Harry responded. "I don't drive anymore. Had my license taken away last year. DWI."

"Oh, that's too bad," Lina said, and she quickly got off the phone.

But a moment later Lina was sorry and her thoughts from the previous days came rushing back to her. She had asked for someone whom could love her after all, not someone who she could love. And when she'd told him about her breast, he hadn't even flinched. Still, the man didn't even have a driver's license! "What should I do?" she asked Gordon, whom she'd been scolding before Harry's call. "You've crossed over to the other side. You must know more about these matters than I do. Would He really expect me to drive up there and pick him up and then drive him back again, you think? Certainly He doesn't want me hanging out at a place like Harold's Gum House. That can't be any good for my soul, and that has to be His main interest at this point."

But the fact of the matter was that He was interested; He had proven that! God had spoken to Lina more directly than He had spoken to anyone she knew of since biblical times. She'd kept it to herself, because even if she found someone who would believe her, they would surely only laugh when they found out what it was He'd communicated. But that was beside the point. He had communicated with her; that was the bottom line. And that was a major event—not only in her life, but in a universal sense.

And so when Harry called back later that evening to say that his boss had agreed to let him take a sick day and that he'd looked at a map and had made some phone calls and could walk the eight miles to the Bearsdon bus depot and then get off in Spotsdale and walk the four miles to Sylvan Estates, there was nothing to say but, "Fine. Try to be here by six."

Still, Lina woke up the next morning at 6:00 a.m. frantic. She'd remembered, between dreams during the night, that she'd told Harry she was rich, as well as sick, and now it seemed entirely possible that that was why he was pursuing her and that God had had nothing to do with any of. And here she'd invited him to her house, a drunk who had no driver's license!

She forced herself to eat breakfast, just to pass some time, and then she dialed Iris's number. But Iris was still sleeping apparently, and Lina didn't leave a message. After she'd showered and dressed, she tried again. This time Iris answered, and when Lina explained that she had to cancel a date with Harry, Iris agreed to call Fred and get the number. But Fred, who was an auto mechanic, was at work of course, and by the time Iris tracked him down (which necessitated calling all six auto service shops in Bearsdon) and got Harry's number and called Lina back to give it to her, it was just past noon, and Harry, who'd estimated that it would take him some six hours to get to Sylvan Estates, had already left.

Lina called Pat next, but Pat, who was working too, told Lina that whatever it was that she was so upset about would have to wait until later. Lina, however, was determined to have the other woman's ear. "Look, Pat," she said. "Do you want to wind up in my will or not?"

"Why, Lina!" Pat exclaimed. "I can't believe you said that! I can't believe you think that I'm motivated by…that my feelings…that I would…Oh, God, Lina!" She went on in this vein for some time, but in the end, after Lina had apologized several times over, Pat told the old woman who was seated in the hydraulic chair that her teeth looked perfect and didn't need to be cleaned after all.

As soon as the woman, who was delighted, left, Lina swore Pat to secrecy and proceeded to tell her everything, beginning with the incident with the fan and the magazine. Pat, who was an atheist, laughed hysterically, and it took Lina some effort to get her to calm down and help. There was nothing to be done about the dinner, Pat said then, but there were some things she could do to keep the brute from thinking that there might be some money in this for him. "Like what?" Lina asked, and when Pat began to enumerate, Lina reached for a pad and a pencil.

As soon as they concluded their conversation, Lina drove to the bank and then to the used car dealership in town, where she purchased an old, dented Chevy, the worst-looking thing on the lot, for cash. For a bit more cash, the proprietor agreed to follow her back to her house with it. Then she parked the Caddy in the garage, locked the garage door, and went out again in the Chevy, to drop off the car dealer and then to go to the Salvation Army, where she purchased an entire outfit, including shoes. Next she went to a discount department store and purchased a wig in the same color as the one she'd been wearing since the onset of the chemo, the difference being that the new one was synthetic, styleless, and poorly made. On the way home, she stopped at the grocery store and picked up the ingredients for the stew that Pat had suggested she make. Once she got it started, she showered again (the Chevy wasn't air-conditioned, and leaving the sweat on her body, though Pat had suggested that too, was more than she could bring herself to do), dressed in her new old clothes, arranged on her head the hideous wig, and hung from her ears the gaudy earrings that Pat had given her some weeks ago.

And just in the nick of time, for the next thing she knew, the door bell was ringing, and then there was Harry standing on her stoop, red-faced, breathless, sweat-drenched, and holding some wilted wildflowers which he had apparently picked along the way. "Harry, how are you?" Lina cried.

Harry, who didn't seem to notice how different she looked, shook his head sorrowfully. "I need a drink."

Lina had no whiskey in the house, but she thought she remembered a bottle of vodka somewhere, and while she searched for it, she told Harry the story that she and Pat had rehearsed. This was, in fact, not her house. She lived out in town, she said, in that nasty section where he'd gotten off the bus. This house belonged to her friend, Sylvia Plath ("Go ahead and say it," Pat had said, laughing. "From what you've told me, he won't as much as blink an eye," and she was right), who was on vacation and had asked Lina to house sit. And so here she was, living in a rich woman's house, wearing her jewelry when she went out—because Sylvia had said that'd be okay—and sort of pretending that she was rich herself, just to see what it was like. "And this Sylvia don't drink, I take it?" Harry asked.

"Apparently not," Lina responded, but then she found the vodka bottle and turned with it, and Harry took a deep breath and whistled on the exhale.

They had their dinner in the kitchen, and Lina, who expected Harry to comment on the beauty of the room, kept turning her head to look at it herself, but Harry only ate his stew and when Lina looked at him directly, smiled. "Tell me about yourself," she said at last.

Harry shrugged. "I work at Bearsdon Manufacturing, doing custodial. I've got three daughters, one married and two still at home— that's Janie, age seventeen, and Gail, age ten. The married one, Beth Ann, is pregnant. Wife died nine years ago, of cancer, but not like what you've got. Hers was lower, if you know what I mean."

"My God," Lina said.

Harry nodded. "Raised the girls myself, pretty much. And didn't manage to do half the job I planned."

"Are they bad girls?" Lina ventured.

Harry laughed. "Oh, no. They're good girls, all three of them, good as gold. I managed that somehow. It's me that got screwed up along the way." He shrugged again.

"You mean the drinking?" Lina asked.

Harry nodded and returned to his stew. But Lina only stared into her own bowl, as horrified as if she were seeing a creature floating in it. What she was actually seeing at that moment is that if it took Harry six hours to get to her house, it would take him six more to get home, and that was if the buses ran at night, which was surely not the case. He had tricked her; either he had come with the intention of staying over, or he was assuming that she would drive him back. "Harry," she said, "have you thought about how you'll get home tonight?"

He swiped his napkin across his mouth and cleared his throat. "Got it all worked out. Carl, that's Beth Ann's husband, gets off work at two. I told him where I was off to, and nice boy that he is, he offered to come out here and pick me up. But I said, 'Carl, this woman ain't going to want me hanging around till no two in the morning.' So we planned that I'd leave here at eleven and walk to the Spotsdale depot and get the last bus out, which leaves at half past twelve. Should get me to the Bearsdon depot at half past one, and then I'll only have another half hour or so to wait till Carl comes for me. Pass me that vodka bottle if you'd please."

"But what time do you have to get up in the morning for work?"

"Five or so. The girls will see to it. Mind if I ask you what's in this stew?"

Lina had not planned to serve dessert (Pat had said that would only encourage him), but in view of all the walking that Harry had done and the walk that he still had ahead of him, she thought he might need the calories and removed a Sara Lee from the freezer. While they waited for it to defrost, they talked some more, or rather, Lina asked questions and Harry answered. She suspected that he was making a great effort not to drink as much as he usually did, for although his gaze kept sweeping toward the vodka bottle, he asked for it only twice more, and once Lina had put the coffee on and cleared the bottle from the table, he didn't say a word about it.

Later, in the living room, he showed Lina a photograph of his girls, all three of them chubby and with stringy brown hair. The little one, he told her, was interested in chemistry, the middle one in boys, and the married one, now that she was pregnant and it was, in Harry's opinion, too late to alter her future, wanted to go to nursing school. Harry shook his head. The girls, he confessed, exhausted him.

"Why me?" Lina asked.

Harry blinked at her.

"You must meet plenty of women over there at (she cringed in preparation for the saying of it) Harold's Gum House," she explained. "And surely most of them live right in your neighborhood and dating them doesn't require taking off a day from work and then traveling more hours than it would take to fly to China."

"Oh, that," Harry said, and he looked away, at the books on Lina's shelves.

"Something inside you," he whispered at last. "Something good I saw the first time you smiled."

Lina didn't remember smiling. "What exactly?" she persisted.

Harry shrugged and let his gaze return to the books. "I could read all them," he said, "and I probably still wouldn't know how to say it right. But I'll give it a try." He thought for a moment, with his lips pursed and his fingers pulling at his chin. "You know the way you look at a pup sometimes, just look him in the eye and you know that he's not going to be one of those slap-happy dogs that chases cars and chews up everything in the house?"

Lina didn't, but she nodded anyway.

"Well, I looked at you and I said to myself, Harry, this is the kind of woman could make you feel like a man again." And his brows shot up, as if his admission had startled him.

When Harry phoned at the end of the week, to see if he could come by again on the weekend, Lina put forth some conditions. If he accepted them, she'd decided, she would assume that their relationship might yet be fated and hang in for a second round. He couldn't drink, she told him, and he'd have to spend some time sitting alone in the bedroom after dinner because she had something she had to do in the kitchen, something that she'd neglected the last time but could not put off again. She hoped he wouldn't ask what it was, and he didn't, but he did ask her if he could have just one drink with dinner, if he promised to sip, and Lina acquiesced.

Harry was able to get a ride right to her house on Saturday, and Lina, who was watching from the window, caught a glimpse of Carl and Beth Ann as they pulled into her driveway in their old pickup truck to drop him off. Harry stood with his hand in the air as they backed out again, and as if he would be away for an inordinate amount of time, Carl beeped the horn several times, and then, just before they took off, Beth Ann leaned over him, stuck her head out the window, and yelled, "Have a good time, Daddy!"

Lina ran to the door and ushered him in. "Harry," she cried, out of breath, "you mustn't do that. In a neighborhood like this, you can't make a lot of noise." She closed the door behind him and ran back to the window to see whether there were any faces in the windows across the street at Carol's house, which there weren't. (Carol had been over during the week, inquiring about the dilapidated Chevy in the driveway. It belonged to a friend of her sister's, a woman who was away in California for the summer, Lina had lied. And since Trish was so busy working and Lina had free time on her hands, Lina had agreed to take it, start it up now and then so that the battery wouldn't die. Carol had shuddered. "I didn't know your sister had such abject connections," she'd said. Lina hadn't told her about Harry and didn't intend to, and when Pat had come over to take her to chemo and asked how it had gone with the money-monger, Lina had said that it went as planned and that she didn't expect to hear from him again.)

"I'm sorry," Harry said. "I'll explain to them. They don't know about neighborhoods like this one. How could they?"

Lina had intended to make Harry something special this time, but she had been sick to her stomach all day and had only managed a salad. She could see that Harry was disappointed, though of course he said nothing about it. She wished he would ask her about the chemo, about what it was like to be nauseous half the time, but she knew by now that, unless he were drunk, he wasn't likely to ask her anything ever. "There's a reason why were having salad tonight," she said finally, and when Harry looked up, whisking a julienned carrot into his mouth with the tip of his tongue, Lina proceeded to tell him all about it. He listened intently, nodding sometimes, probably where the particulars corresponded with his recollections of his wife's illness, and wincing others, so that Lina imagined that this untutored man was nevertheless able to feel some compassion for her ordeal.

Afterwards, Harry offered to help clean up, but Lina reminded him that she'd told him that she had to be alone after dinner, and he allowed her to escort him up to the bedroom. She left him sitting on

125

the edge of the bed with his hands folded on his lap and his head swiveling to take in the various paintings, most of which were floral, that lined the walls. Then she returned to the kitchen, determined that evening to have it out with Gordon over the occasion of the last anniversary they'd had together. She hadn't expected a gift, but a card would have been nice, or at least some acknowledgment that it was their anniversary. But Gordon had only grunted when she gave him her card, and when she went into his room the next day after he'd left for work (as she did often, searching for—but never finding—some clue to his behavior among his credit cards receipts and the other scraps of paper that accumulated on his dresser), she found the envelope, which had never been opened, in his waste paper basket. "You were so cruel, Gordon," she said softly, just in case Harry had opened the door and was trying to listen.

Ordinarily, it brought Lina some satisfaction to speak to Gordon this way. She worked so hard on visualizing him sitting there, squirming, dying to say his piece, but entirely unable, that sometimes she almost thought she saw him. But the knowledge that there was a man sitting in her bedroom, a man who seemed to think that something could be gained by loving her, distracted her, and she found herself looking over her shoulder, towards the stairs that led to him, instead of at Gordon. "Enough said," she said firmly, and she got up briskly and went to rescue Harry.

They watched a movie together that night, a comedy called *Groundhog Day*, which made them both laugh. Harry had a habit of lunging forward when something struck him funny, just the way Gordon used to do. (It was probably the only thing the two had in common, and watching him, Lina felt a pang, a genuine response to Gordon's absence.) Harry seemed to enjoy himself, and if he was thinking about the little bit of vodka that was left in the bottle, he showed no sign of it. At eleven, when Carl and Beth Ann were due to come and get him, Harry volunteered to wait outside in the driveway so that they would see him right away and wouldn't have to beep. Lina was hoping he would kiss her goodnight, for the truth was that he had one of those faces that grew on you, a healthy face, round and virtually unlined, with eyes that were clear and blue. But he only tipped an invisible hat to her and went out the door.

She might have turned on the outdoor lights, but as she didn't want to call anyone's attention to him, she let him stand in the dark. Still, the moonlight enabled her to observe him through the window, and what she saw was that he was so intent on flagging down Carl before he could beep that twice he stepped off the curb unnecessarily and flung an arm in the air in response to an approaching car. Otherwise he stood motionlessly, for a full half hour, never as much as turning his head to look back at the house.

All the following week Lina thought about him. Of all the men that she had met since Gordon's demise, he was the least interesting, or at least by her former standards he was, and yet she couldn't get him out of her mind. She had no urge to speak to Gordon that week, and she imagined that in his disgust he had picked up and left her, and although there were still many matters which she had not yet discussed with him, she was glad.

Harry called on Friday and said that he could get a ride out on Saturday, but it would have to be in the morning because Carl and Beth Ann were going to visit Carl's parents in New Jersey for the weekend, and would it be an imposition for Lina to have him around all day. "Not at all," Lina said, "but if Carl and Beth Ann are going to be away for the weekend, how will you get home?"

As usual, Harry had an elaborate plan. If he left at six in the evening, he could be at the Spotsdale depot by seven-thirty, and then he could take the bus not to Bearsdon but to the town of Butler, where his friend James was going to be installing a satellite dish for someone until about nine. Then James would drive him home and save him the long walk from the Bearsdon depot to his house. "Why don't you just stay over?" Lina suggested.

"Stay what?"

Lina laughed. "Stay overnight."

"At Sylvia's house?"

"Yes, here. And I'll drive you back in the morning."

Harry was silent. "Hello?" Lina said. "Hello, Harry, are you still there?"

He laughed. "I think so. I think I am."

They had a picnic lunch that day. Lina had wanted to drive up into the mountains, but she was afraid that the Chevy wouldn't make it, so they went to a park a few miles south of Spotsdale and watched the children there chase geese while they ate. Harry was particularly quiet, and Lina thought he must be wondering whether her invitation was a seduction or simply a matter of convenience that would result in him being put up in the guest room. She was wondering that herself. She had been to see Claire during the week, and she had told her about Harry. To her astonishment, Claire hadn't been enthusiastic at all. "You told him you were rich and you told him you were sick," she'd said. "How can you be so certain that he isn't after your money?" Lina had explained about the car and the fabrication concerning the house then, but Claire remained unsettled. "He can't be that stupid," she'd said. "It's a cover up, Lina."

Lina intended to cook that night, something light since they'd had such a big lunch, but Harry wouldn't hear of it. He hadn't been to Harold's Gum House all week, he said, and he wanted to use the money he'd saved to take her out to dinner. "You mean you haven't been drinking?" Lina asked.

"That's right. I'm sober," Harry declared, and he smiled. Then he cocked his head from side to side in a way that was now becoming familiar to Lina. "Well, kind of sober. I did have one this morning, before I left the house." He hesitated and then murmured under his breath, "Cause of being…you know…nervous."

They went to a Chinese restaurant, where Lina had only some shrimp fried rice and Harry had three orders of spare ribs, the excellence of which he exclaimed over all the while he ate. On the way home they picked up a video, *A Fish Called Wanda*, because Lina felt like laughing again. But just as they were about to settle down and watch it, the doorbell rang, and thinking that it could only be Pat or Carol, Lina panicked. "Run up to the bedroom," she ordered, jumping to her feet.

Harry looked at her, and she saw that she had hurt him. "Just for a moment," she added. "Until I see who it is."

Harry sighed and got up and Lina rushed to the door. "Lina!" Carol cried. "I came by earlier, and you weren't home."

"I was out," Lina said flatly.

"Out in the Chevy?" She stretched her neck to see beyond Lina. "Aren't you going to ask me in?"

"I was just going to bed."

"It's only nine. That's not like you. And why are you wearing those rags? And what have you done to your hair? Your wig? Are you okay?

Are you depressed? Because if you are, that makes two of us. Gloria sprained her wrist today doing cartwheels, and then J.J. stuck his hand in a hole in the backyard and got bitten by something, but he didn't know what it was and we had to—"

"Carol," Lina interrupted. "I have company."

Carol's jaw dropped. "A man?"

"Yes, Carol."

Carol tried to look past her again, but Lina eased the door forward until it was nearly closed and whispered, "Goodnight."

As soon as Carol had gone, Lina raced to the bedroom where she found Harry standing in the near dark, holding a framed photograph of her and Trish. It had been taken ten years ago, when Lina was a happier woman. The two sisters, who were laughing in the photo, had their arms around each other and their heads close together. Harry put it back on the dresser. "I'm sorry," Lina said, but she could think of nothing to add by way of explanation.

Harry cocked his head toward the photo he'd been holding. "That Sylvia?"

"Yes," Lina lied.

"You look alike," he muttered.

"I suppose."

Harry shook his head. "I don't want to watch the fish movie anymore," he said sadly.

Lina, who was on the verge of tears, whispered, "I don't blame you."

The two stood staring at each other, scrutinizing each other's eyes, Lina thinking that she didn't deserve Harry's love, if that was what it was, that she was glad now that this had happened, that her wickedness had been revealed, for what was the point in having someone fall in love with you when you were only going to die? "I'm dying," she said finally.

Harry flinched. "I know."

She forced a laugh. "And I keep thinking that being so close to death should make me a better person, but that's not what's happening at all."

"You're not a bad person," Harry said. "You're a good person. A very good one."

"Good?" asked Lina. She couldn't think what she had done to give him that impression.

Harry opened his mouth to elaborate but then whispered, "Come here."

Lina took a step, tentatively, still watching his face for some clue as to what he was thinking. One step farther and she could see that there were tears in his eyes too, and she wondered if it was his wife who was on his mind. She took a third step and whispered, "I'm here."

"So am I," he whispered back, and taking a deep breath through his nose, he lifted his hands into the air, then lowered them onto Lina's shoulders. Then, with his eyes still penetrating hers, he let his right hand slide down the front of her shirt.

Lina laughed lightly and quickly lifted his hand away. "That's the wrong one," she said. "That's the prosthesis." She saw his features contort ruefully, but before he could say anything, she placed his large, callused, trembling hand on the real one.

Lina awoke in Harry's arms, and if she had ever been happier in her life, she didn't remember it. They had talked during the night, in

131

addition to the other, really talked, lying side by side and hand in hand in the dark. Not that Harry had been verbose, exactly. But he had answered enough of her questions so that she was able to piece together certain aspects of his life. He had grown up on a river somewhere north of Buffalo, the youngest of three boys. His passion in his youth had been fly fishing, and he admitted that he'd skipped plenty of school days to pursue it. He had loved the quiet of it, the peacefulness, the feeling of being alone with nature. And his wife, Suzanne, had produced much the same emotions in him, because she had been a quiet woman, inwardly peaceful, who cared for her house and her children (and Harry too, he'd said) with an unflappable conviction. She had known somehow, intuitively, when the girls would recuperate on their own and when they needed the care of a doctor. Likewise, when Harry first began drinking, she knew when to flush him out with coffee and insist on an explanation and when it was best to leave him alone—though of course the really serious drinking didn't begin until after her passing.

Lina had talked about her life too, particularly her years with Gordon. She'd told Harry how he'd turned on her, and all because he'd had a little ulcer. ("He was scared," Harry had said. "But he'd had no real reason to be," Lina had countered. "Don't matter," Harry had replied. "Ever hold a stick up in front of a strange dog? May be your intention's not to hit him at all, but he don't know that. When people are scared, they get vicious." "Then what should I have done?" Lina had asked. "Should have held him till he stopped struggling." "Is that what you did," Lina had said, "with Suzanne?" "No," Harry had answered, "that's what she did with me. She was the one dying and I was the one scared." "Then I failed him," Lina had whispered, but Harry had only put his arms around her and whispered something about her being incapable of doing anything but her very best. And when she broke, sobbing continuously for nearly an hour, unleashing all the pain that she had been carrying around with her for so long, he only held her tighter.)

Lina imagined disentangling herself, slipping into her robe and going out into the kitchen and making him the most incredible breakfast he had ever had in his life, but she couldn't bring herself to alter the moment one iota. And then he awoke, and as soon as he saw her, he smiled and told her to get dressed because he had a little surprise for her waiting at his house, but when she went to move, he wouldn't let her go.

His house was an older one, with no yard to speak of, and the pavement leading to the door was cracked and uneven, as was the stoop. Harry rang the doorbell, which surprised Lina, but then it occurred to her that it must be part of the surprise, and she waited beside him in silence for a full five minutes, breathing in the aroma of bacon, until the door was finally opened.

The face behind it was Gail's, the ten-year-old's. Lina noticed that her glasses were uncommonly thick and her braids were held together with blue rubber bands. "Welcome to Harry's Diner," she said somberly, but then there was a snort of laughter from within, and Gail reacted to it by bucking forward and slapping her palm over her mouth.

When she'd recovered, she swung the door open and stood back, and then the older one, Janie, came forward wearing a bright red apron. Her hair, which must have been much longer than it had been in the picture, was done up in a bun at the top of her head. Her eyes were blue like Harry's, and her skin was so white as to be nearly transparent. She wasn't exactly pretty (her teeth were large and she didn't have much of a chin), but her neck was long and she was thinner than she'd been in the photo. "Good morning, sir, ma'am," she said, looking down and trembling with repressed laughter, and she handed them each a sheet of loose leaf paper on which the breakfast menu had been written in an ornate purple script.

"Why, thank you, miss," Lina declared, and Janie flashed a smile.

They followed the girls through the living room (which was tidy, but otherwise—with its cheap pine furniture and colorlessness— unimpressive) and into the kitchen, where the table had been set with an unironed cloth and dishes that didn't match and a wine bottle full of wildflowers. While Gail closed the blinds Janie lit the candles, and then the girls hurried to pull out two chairs and seat their guests. "Aren't you going to eat with us?" Lina asked.

"No," said Gail. "We're just the staff and we don't mingle." She had barely gotten the last word out when she had to clap her palm over her mouth to keep from giggling again.

That evening, Lina invited Pat and Carol over for tea and the pastries that she'd picked up on the way home from Harry's house. "I've met a man," she said as soon as the two were seated.

"Apparently," said Carol, who was still miffed after having had the door closed in her face the night before.

Lina ignored her and turned to Pat, who was poking through the pastries. "It's the one I told you about. I lied to you. I didn't get rid of him."

"You can't mean it!" Pat cried, her hand withdrawing from the tray in haste. "The money-monger? The ignorant, drunken brute you met at the country western bar?"

"What's this?" cried Carol. "Pat knows all about this and I was told nothing?"

Lina placed an apple fritter on her plate, dispensed with her tea bag, and added a spoonful of honey to her cup. The other two, realizing that she would not speak until they'd calmed down, followed suit. Then, when Pat and Carol had begun to nibble and sip, Lina told the story, slowly and from the beginning, but so as not to elicit any laughter from Carol, leaving out the part about the fan and the magazine, which, fortunately, Pat had the good sense not to mention either. "Aren't you happy for me?" she asked at last.

"You're settling, " Carol said smugly. She pushed her plate aside and patted her mouth with her napkin. "You have nothing in common with this person. You're assuming that because of your condition, you can't do any better, but I happen to think you can."

"And this thing with his daughters," Pat began as soon as Carol broke off, "it's outrageous, Lina. Can't you see that? A man doesn't bring his lover around so quickly to meet his kids…unless he wants something. And the flowers, and them waiting on you hand and foot…Of course he's treating you like a queen, because he knows you're wealthy and he wants…Oh, Lina, don't make me say it! Don't make me spell it out for you!"

But she did spell it out over the course of the next hour. They both did. And though Lina appreciated their concern (if that was what it was), she refused to believe that Harry was anything less than madly in love with her.

He called her every night now. She'd saved him, he said. If not for her, he'd be at Harold's Gum House instead of home helping Gail with her summer school homework and making sure that Janie (who was also in summer school but who didn't do homework) went out dressed like a lady and with lady-like friends. He was a father again, thanks to her. And a better worker too, now that he didn't have to go in each morning with his head dull from the night before. He'd always imagined that it would be difficult, if not impossible, to stop drinking. But now he saw that all it took was wanting to please someone more than you wanted to please yourself. And each night Lina would reply that it was the other way around, that he had saved her, because she was feeling stronger by the day and thought that she might be able to beat this thing after all. But Harry never made any comment at all to that, so that Lina began to think that either he didn't believe it was possible for her to heal, or, when the doubts that Pat and Carol and Claire had initiated crept in, that he didn't want it to be possible, that maybe it didn't coincide with his plans.

But the doubts crept in infrequently, and most of the time Lina believed what she wanted to believe, for it was a fact that she did feel better, and if Harry's love had been anything short of authentic, then how could it have such a restorative effect?

She had her blood tested, and when she went to see her doctor again, she felt certain that he would confirm that the turmoil within was subsiding. While she waited to speak to him, she thought of the Kitchen Exquisite ad, and how, with a little bit of effort, her kitchen had been remodeled to look just like it. And of course she thought of the Sundown ad, and how that too had come to pass. You needed a picture in your head; it was as simple as that. She had worked on visualization exercises for months on end with Claire, but the picture that Claire had helped her to create had been shadowy and remote. Now she had a picture of health, happiness, and a future with Harry and his daughters (she had found the two younger ones to be charming, sweet and unassuming, and while she had no desire to be a mother to them at this stage, she was as anxious to soak up their affections as she was their father's), and she didn't see how the results of her test could be anything but confluent with it. Yet, when Doctor Peterson finally came into the room, there was a look of concern on his face. And Lina, who had been smiling the moment before, unconsciously modified her own features accordingly. "What?" she asked.

"You're not responding to the chemicals anymore," he said.

"But that's not possible."

"It doesn't mean that we're giving up hope, Lina," he went on. "We're just going to have to wait a few weeks, give your blood cells a chance to rest, and then, as soon as we see some evidence that you're ready for it, we'll start you on a different combination of chemicals."

"What if I don't respond to them?" Lina asked weakly.

"Well, then we'll have to see."

The weekend came and brought Harry with it. He got out of Carl's pickup late Saturday morning with a dozen long-stemmed red roses, and Lina, recalling the first time he had arrived with the wilted wildflowers, wondered whether this was a token of commitment or connivance. She mumbled a thank you and stuck them into a vase without bothering to arrange them. Over lunch she told him the details of her week, watching his face especially closely when she got to the part about the chemicals having stopped working. But he only continued to lunge at his roast beef sandwich, and she couldn't tell whether he was ignorant of the ramifications of that or merely indifferent. Then, after they'd eaten and Harry had answered her questions concerning his and the girls' activities during the week, it occurred to Lina that all she had to do to get at the truth for once and for all was to inform Harry that under no circumstances would he find himself in her will. "When I went to see my lawyer this week," she began cautiously, "I had her draw up my will in such a way that all my possessions would be divided equally among my sister and my two friends, Carol and Pat." (In fact, she had finally gone to see a lawyer, a young, pretty, business-like woman by the name of Mary Jones. And she had divided up some, at least, of her possessions between Carol and Pat. Since Carol liked to read and was always admiring Lina's mahogany book shelves, Lina was leaving her both the shelves and their contents. The jewelry she was leaving Pat. But as it seemed unfair that Pat should get something of so much more monetary value than Carol—and as Lina didn't want to be held responsible in the afterlife for stirring up any more jealousy than already existed between the two women—she had added some cash to the collection of books so that the total value of both gifts would be more or less the same. The lawyer had sighed meanwhile, and though she was getting $220 an hour, had rested her head on her palm and her elbow on the desk so that Lina came to feel foolish and decided she had better go home and think things over before she went any further.)

Harry, who was using the sides of his hands to gather his crumbs into an ever-tightening circle at the center of his plate, said nothing.

"Not that I have that much to divide," Lina went on. "If I owned this place and had the kind of money that Sylvia has, it would have been a lot more difficult deciding."

"I 'spose," said Harry, not lifting his eyes.

"Anyway, I guess it's good not to have too much at a time like this," she persisted.

"You got more than you're admitting," Harry said, glancing up from his circle of crumbs with one eyebrow raised.

"What!" cried Lina, stricken.

He got up from his chair then and came behind hers and bent to put his arms around her. "You got assets nobody knows about," he whispered, and he kissed her neck.

Lina squirmed and Harry promptly released her. "Well, I can't leave those to anyone, can I?" she asked shrilly.

Harry's lower lip jutted forward and he blew air out of his mouth. "I upset you. What'd I do?"

But it dawned on her then that the man had just given her a lovely compliment. "It's me, Harry," she said finally. "I'm moody as hell today."

Harry laughed.

"What's so funny?" Lina snapped.

"Nothing. Just never heard you curse before."

Unfortunately, this incident did not put an end to Lina's suspicions for very long, for if Gordon's lack of love had brought on her illness, then Harry's love, had it been genuine, should have saved her, and here she was dying anyway. She was having her blood tested more frequently now, and each time Dr. Peterson gave her the same bad news; her red blood cell count was still too low; until it built back up, the chemicals were not an option.

Lina continued to take every opportunity to put Harry's love to the test. He came over one weekend complaining of a headache, and she harped on him until she got him to admit that he had been out drinking with Fred the night before. It was the first time since he'd quit, and the last, he assured her, but she lectured him on the perils of alcohol nonetheless—for his own good, she said, though what she was really seeking to do was to determine how much control she had over his life, over his love for her. Nor did she stop there. She made comments about the clothes he wore, about the fact that his shirts were seldom ironed and that all his pants were somewhat too short. She interrogated him about the girls, and when she learned that while Gail was doing well in summer school, Janie's grades were slipping, she demanded to know what Harry proposed to do about that. And when he opened his palms and asked, "What can I do?" she admonished him for being an unconcerned parent, for not even having made an attempt to keep the girl in on week nights and see whether that would help. Then, as if he'd been the one to bring up the subject, she chided him for speaking so often about the girls, about every day affairs, about what he'd eaten for lunch, and the things that happened on the job. The world was bigger than that, she said (though her own interest in the world at large had dwindled with the onset of her illness). Had he no interest in worldly affairs? In esoteric matters? But Harry only shrugged.

Between the walking to and from bus depots (which was often still necessary) and the sobriety, Harry eventually began to lose weight. Pat and Carol had expressed a desire to meet him on several occasions, but Lina put it off until Harry's paunch was almost completely gone. And then, on the morning of the day that they were to come over, she sat Harry down at the kitchen table and lectured him on the subject of noun and verb agreement, the lack of which was his greatest grammatical offense. He claimed to understand, but later that afternoon, and not five minutes before Carol and Pat were due to arrive, Lina happened to ask him how Fred and Iris were doing, and Harry answered, "Was doing fine last I heard."

Exasperated, Lina jumped up from the couch. "Were," she cried. "They were doing fine."

Harry's brows shot up. "Yeah, that's what I said."

Lina threw her hands up in despair. She was on the verge of telling him that his best bet was to say as little as possible, but somehow she managed to restrain herself. Still, Harry eventually gleaned the nature of his error (if not the error itself), and when Pat and Carol arrived (fortunately, they had been invited only for tea), he answered their questions with monosyllables and glancing at Lina constantly for some indication that he was doing okay, which she was not inclined to give him.

Lina would not let him near her that night. She clung to the edge of the bed and told herself that Carol had been right, that she had settled because of her illness and would never have entertained the idea of dating someone like him had she been well. She had fought so hard, after the loss of her breast and her hair, to hang on to what little self-esteem she had left (and after her ordeal with Gordon, it wasn't much) and now she felt it slipping again, and she blamed that on Harry.

She'd promised to drive him home in the morning, but when he awoke she said that the Chevy had been acting up and that she didn't want to risk a break down. Harry professed to understand perfectly, and in the course of the conversation that followed, he admitted that he'd had some reservations about the Chevy himself. He suggested that Lina think about buying a new car. Lina, who took this as confirmation that Harry was well aware that she could easily afford one, snapped at him. "I love my car," she cried. "I've had it for years. It has sentimental value. I wouldn't think of buying a new one even if I could afford it. It just needs a new battery, that's all."

"Well," Harry responded, "we could take it over to Fred's on the way to my house and he could install a battery for you. That'd be a solution."

"No," Lina shouted into his perplexed face. "I've got a stomachache. I can't possibly drive you home."

He blinked at her for a moment, then asked to use the phone to check on the bus schedule. Lina went to hand him the cordless, but he said that he didn't want to disturb her, and after dressing hastily, he went to use the one in the kitchen. Lina, meanwhile, got up and cracked the door. "No," she heard him say, "she ain't coming…No, I won't be eating neither…No…No…No. No sense in saving it. It'll take me too long."

As it happened, Lina did feel sick to her stomach that day, though she didn't realize it until later, after Harry had gone and she had made an attempt at a slice of buttered toast. The nausea too she blamed on Harry, on the fact that he had upset her. And when he called in the early evening, to say that he had just gotten in and wanted to know if she was feeling any better, she told him that she was thinking that maybe it had been a mistake for them to come together in her eleventh hour, and when he asked her what she meant by that, she promptly hung up on him. He called her back and apologized for whatever it was that he had done wrong, but Lina, who took his persistence in the face of her incivility to be yet more evidence that Carol and Pat and Claire had been right, only hung up on him again.

142

Lina felt no better the next day nor the one after that, and when three days had gone by without her being able to eat anything more than a couple of crackers, she took the Caddy out of the garage and went to see Dr. Peterson. He gave her some more tests and determined that he would have to put her into the hospital where she could be fed intravenously until the trouble passed. "Is this it?" she dared to ask him.

"It may be, Lina."

Claire and Pat and Carol and Iris and Trish were only a few of the people who came to visit Lina in the hospital. The entire staff at the Community Center came, and some of Gordon's colleagues as well. Most of her neighbors from Sylvan Estates showed up, many of whom she had never had more than brief conversations with before. She had some cousins on Long Island, and they came too, as did an Aunt from Minnesota and an Uncle from Texas whom she hadn't seen in years. And as if they could make up for the fact that Lina was now down to the bare essentials (the nurses had removed her prosthesis and replaced her wig with a cotton turban), each and every one of her guests brought a gift. Within three days there was no more room on the window ledge and the nurses had to line up the flower arrangements that were still arriving on the floor beneath it. The night table filled up with cards and music boxes and books (both inspirational and otherwise) and crystals and bells and candles and every other sort of trinket. The nurses made jokes about it; they said that Lina would have to rent a U-haul in order to get everything home. But Lina knew very well that she was never going home, and even if she were, there was nothing in the room that she would want to take with her. She had only one concern now, and, surprisingly enough, it was not the prospect of her demise. No; except for her brief time with Harry, she had long been ambivalent regarding her death, as people are when they are miserable much of the time, and she had already given it much more thought than it deserved. Now that it was imminent, she found it impossible to focus on it for more than a moment or two at a time. Of far more interest was the one thing that was no longer available to her: Food.

When she slept, she dreamed about thick corned beef sandwiches on rye bread with pickles on the side or bowls of pasta with rich Italian sauces. She dreamed of pastries and dumplings and ribs and puddings and fat steaks smothered in onions and all the other rich, fatty foods that she had seldom allowed herself to indulge in. And each time she awakened to find that she had yet another visitor, she tried to engage him or her in a conversation about the foods she had dreamed of, but her guests all had the same response: First they looked at Lina with faces contorted with sympathy. Then they looked at the IV, which was now her only source of nourishment. And finally they changed the subject, either to report some cheerful anecdote that Lina had to force herself to respond to or, as if it would alleviate them, to probe Lina on the matter of her discomforts.

She was in the hospital well over a week when Harry called. No one had bothered to tell him that Lina had been hospitalized, and he was very upset. Since she had hung up on him the last time he'd spoken to her, he'd thought it best to wait a few days before trying again, and then when he did try and couldn't reach her, he assumed that she was simply not answering the phone so as not to have to speak to him. But when three or four more days had passed and he still hadn't got an answer, he got worried and took a day off from work and walked to the Bearsdon depot and took the bus to Spotsdale and walked to Sylvan Estates and sat outside her house, taking shelter in the Chevy when it began to pour, and waited around for her until it was time to walk back to the Spotsdale depot and catch the last bus for home. Finally, he called Fred, but Fred and Iris had had an argument (over Fred's dancing with another woman half the night the last time they had been to Harold's Gum House), and Fred refused to call her to see what she knew. Then Harry remembered that Pat and Carol lived in the neighborhood, and he took another day off to return to Sylvan Estates with the intention of going door to door until he found one of them. But no one was home behind the first four doors, and he was just beginning to think that maybe the whole neighborhood had been evacuated for some reason he couldn't imagine when a little girl went by on a bicycle. He called to her, and when she turned and peddled back to him, he asked her about Carol and Pat. The child replied that except for the kids, she knew the neighbors by their last names only, Mr. This and Mrs. That, and if there was a Pat or a Carol in Sylvan Estates, she didn't know anything about it. Harry was about to let her go on her way again when it occurred to him to ask her where her own house was, for he was thinking now that he would go and question her mother. And when the child informed him that her mother had gone to visit some neighbor, some sick woman in the hospital, Harry knew what had happened.

Still, it had taken a further effort for him to locate Lina, for the child wasn't sure which hospital the sick woman was in. Harry had to go home again and call every hospital in two counties, and of course with his luck, Lina was in the last one on the list. "Well, you've found me now," Lina, who could no longer remember what had possessed her to hang up on him, said.

"Thank God," Harry whispered.

Harry said he wanted to visit, but the hospital that Lina was in was forty miles south of Spotsdale, which meant that it was eighty miles south of Bearsdon, and Harry had not yet figured out how to get there. He was working on it, he declared; where there was a will, there was a way, and he would sure as hell find it. "In the meantime," he said, "what can I do for you?"

"Tell me what you had for lunch today," Lina said.

Harry hesitated. "Carrot sticks," he said at last.

"Harry," Lina sang in warning.

Harry sighed. "Two burgers, an order of fries, and a quart of chocolate milk."

"You're kidding," Lina cried. "I was just thinking about fries before you called."

"You mean you're not going to say nothing about me not trying to keep my weight down?"

"Why would I say that?"

"Cause you been telling me I shouldn't eat grease for weeks now."

"I said that?" Lina asked, concerned to think that her memory might go before her body did.

"Yeah, you did. That's a fact."

Harry was determined to find a way to get down there, but it would be difficult. He had used up all his sick days already, and he might have gotten Carl and Beth Ann to drive him over on the weekend, but some complications had arisen in Beth Ann's pregnancy, and her doctor, who was located some distance north of Bearsdon, wanted the couple to stay close by. He sought out a direct bus route

146

of course, but in those rural counties there weren't many bus routes to begin with, and the best indirect route that he could find would have left him with a twenty-mile hike between depots. Lina swiped at his excuses with a weak arm. "It doesn't matter," she said, "as long as we're able to communicate."

As his job required only physical exertion, Harry had plenty of time to think, and what he thought about was food, because that was what Lina had asked him to do. When he took his break each morning, he called her and described the dishes that had come to mind. Afternoon break he did the same thing. Then he called her again after dinner and told her what he and Gail and Janie had had. Lina would question him then, asking him who had done the cooking (the three took turns) and how each item had been prepared and who had eaten how much of what and so forth. And though he labored to get the details right, there were still times when his descriptions (especially where the taste of a particular item was concerned) were lacking, and then she would ask him to put one of the girls on the phone. Gail giggled a lot, but her knowledge of chemistry was impressive, and she used it to enhance her descriptions. Janie took the matter much more seriously, because she was dieting and had her own food fixations, but her descriptions of the taste of a thing were usually not much better than her father's—though she was able to describe the colors of various foods well enough when they corresponded to the different colors of nail polish she wore.

Lina lived for his calls, literally. Whether he loved her or not was no longer important to her; her cancer had metastasized by then, and she was too weak to bother with ephemeral matters. Furthermore, the morphine that Dr. Peterson had added to her IV only enhanced her food dreams and her desire for food, and Harry was the only one who seemed to understand that. Sometimes when he called she wasn't up to conversation at all, but Harry understood that too, and then he answered the questions he knew she would have been asking had she been able. Thus, whether asleep or awake, Lina envisioned smorgasbords overflowing with hot dogs and beans and juicy hamburgers and all the other foods that Harry and his daughters ate.

One afternoon a nurse came in carrying a package the size of a shoe box. Lina, certain that it was yet another trinket, waved her arm to indicate that the nurse should take it straight away. She had been thinking about jelly beans, of all things, going through the various colors and attempting to recall the flavor of each. She had been stuck on green when the nurse entered; she simply couldn't envision the flavor of that one. Still, she thought that if she held the image in her head long enough, the recollection would come to her, and she resented the nurse's interruption. The nurse, however, was one of those perky types who believe their forced cheerfulness can't be anything but a balm to their patients, and she bounced down on the edge of the bed (so that both the mattress and Lina bobbed in response) and proceeded to open the package anyway. "What do you suppose could be in this one?" she squealed as she pulled at the string and tore away the brown wrapper. She shook the box. "It's very light. You want to shake it?"

"No, I don't," Lina said tartly, but the nurse, who was used to sour responses, ignored her and shook the box again, this time near her ear. Then she drew her shoulders up and in, so that she looked like a turtle, and taking a deep breath, she lifted the lid and peeked. Her smile fell away instantly. "Is this someone's idea of a joke?" she asked.

"Let me see," said Lina, and she reached for the box.

The nurse pulled it away. "Someone's got a very warped sense of humor," she snapped, and clutching the box to her chest, she started up from the bed. Lina, however, managed to get hold of her sleeve, and when she yanked, the box tilted, and its contents, several hundred magazine clippings from *Gourmet* and *Better Homes and Gardens* and *Lady's Home Journal* cascaded onto the bed.

Mumbling under her breath, the nurse bent to gather them up, but Lina slapped at her hands. "Go away," she shouted. "Go away right now!"

Lina picked up a clipping depicting a jar of Miracle Whip and found that on the bottom, in the same purple ink that Janie had used some weeks ago to write out her menu for the breakfast that she and Gail had served up, Harry had written, "For Lina Wolff, who whips up miracles without even knowing it." She laughed, and when her laughter turned to tears, she closed her eyes and held the clipping to her heart. Then, having regained enough control to go on, she picked up a clipping of a Hunt's Ketchup bottle on which Harry had written, "Lina Wolff is the one I was hunting for." "These look to be the color of your eyes I think," he'd written on a clipping featuring a bunch of green grapes overhanging a wrought iron table edge, and on one showing a quart of strawberries, "These sure look like your lips to me." Some of the clippings were of prepared dishes (Lobster Raffles, Goose Liver in Aspic, Ladyfingers with Blackberry Cream), the likes of which Harry had likely never tasted, and on these he had written nothing. But he had left the fine print beneath each of them intact, and with the purple pen, had underlined the adjectives ("savory," "tangy," "delectable," "appetizing") to which he thought Lina would want to have her attention called.

The nurse reappeared, scowling, and with Dr. Peterson in tow, but Lina was too absorbed to notice them. They watched Lina for a moment. Then Dr. Peterson put his hand on the nurse's shoulder and steered her back toward the hall.

Lina fell asleep clutching a picture of a plate of Noisettes of Lamb to her chest, and when she awoke, some hours later, she was relieved to see she still had it and that the other clippings had been returned to the shoe box and that the shoe box was right there on her tray. She could imagine it—Harry in his kitchen for several evenings in succession, at the table with Janie and Gail on either side of him, going through the magazines the girls had bought, scrutinizing both sides of each page to determine which had the most mouth-watering picture. She could hear the metallic sound of the scissors, and their voices, low and matter-of-fact. Whether she ever saw Harry again or not, it contented her to think that she would leave this world in the state of grace that only the giving and receiving of love enables one to attain. But then another thought arose out of nowhere, some sense that something had been left undone, and when Trish appeared at her bedside a half hour later, Lina remembered what it was. "My will," she moaned (in spite of the morphine, she was in pain at that moment). "Mary Jones."

"Your lawyer," Trish said matter-of-factly.

"Yes. You've got to call her. Got to get her here."

"Darling," whispered Trish, "I don't know how to say this, but you're in no condition to be making changes to your will now."

In her mind's eye Lina saw a half a melon filled with raspberries, centered in a crystal bowl and surrounded by crushed ice. If she closed her eyes, she knew, she would be able to taste the berries. But she fought against the temptation to do so and struggled instead to make sense out of the fact that Trish appeared to know about her lawyer, though she'd never mentioned Ms. Jones to her. She probably knew too then, Lina reasoned, that the will had never been completed, that as next of kin, she would automatically inherit everything. She freed a hand from the sheets and grabbed Trish's wrist. "Please," she begged. "I need to make a change."

"You're on morphine, Lina," Trish explained more harshly. "You can't make changes to your will while you're under the influence of that kind of a drug. It wouldn't be valid."

"Then you've got to do it. You've got to distribute everything the way I say."

Trish sighed. "Okay, what do you want me to do?"

Lina trashed her free hand about. When her voice came, it was shrill. "You need a paper, a pen."

"Just tell me," Trish persisted. "I'll remember. I'll do exactly what you want."

"No," Lina cried. "Witnesses, a pen." She found the buzzer and pressed it and in a moment the perky nurse came rushing in. "Paper, pen!" Lina cried.

Trish smiled at the nurse. "She's having a bad time here," she said gently. "We'll be okay." The nurse smiled back and left, and then Trish poked through her bag and came up with a credit card receipt and the sort of tiny pencil that they give out at miniature golf courses. "Shoot," she said. "I'll write it all down."

"The girls," Lina said. "Harry's girls."

"Oh, yes," Trish interrupted. "Pat and Carol told me all about Harry and his daughters."

Lina was exhausted now, and as the vision of the melon had passed, she closed her eyes and let her head drop back onto the pillow. "Trust funds," she mumbled, "for the two younger ones. Cash for the married one. And the car for Harry, for when he gets his license back." Then she opened her eyes again, but to her astonishment, the room was dark, and the frenzied, scraping sound that she had taken to be Trish's scrawl turned out to be the swish of the nurses' uniforms as they hurried back and forth in the quiet hall.

Harry didn't know anything about the service, which took place two month's after Lina's death, until the night before, when Iris called on Trish's behalf to say that Lina had left him something. Naturally he was curious, and during the course of the night, after he had called his boss to arrange to take off the day and then plotted out a route to the Spotsdale Cemetery, he imagined any number of mementos that would have meaning for him. But he slept restlessly, and when he awoke in the morning he felt relatively certain that Lina's people only wanted to return the shoe box to him, the food clippings. He had spoken to Lina twice more after she'd received it, and both times, in spite of her weakening state, she had managed to let him know how much it meant to her. Then, the last time he'd called her room, another woman had answered and said that Lina was too far gone for phone calls and that he shouldn't bother trying again. After that, he called the nurses' station as regularly as he'd called Lina previously (to give them abbreviated messages concern-ing food, though their impatience led him to doubt that the messages were passed on), and two days later one of the nurses told him that Lina was dead.

As Lina had wanted to be cremated, there'd been no funeral, and Trish, who'd been anxious to clear out the house so that it could be sold as soon as possible, had waited the two months to arrange for the service. It was cool by then, and drizzling that day, and most of the people who gathered together to honor Lina held umbrellas over their heads. The first person to speak was Trish of course, but as she didn't bother to introduce herself to the assemblage (all of whom, with the exception of Harry, already knew who she was), Harry had no way to know this. Still, she seemed vaguely familiar to him. "Lina loved people," Trish said. She was wearing a black and white striped suit that made Harry think of a zebra. "And she loved life, and she clung to it tenaciously right up until the very end."

She appeared to have more to say, but she burst into tears quite suddenly, and another woman came forward and led her away. Then the director from the Community Center, who did introduce herself, stepped into the center of the assemblage and gave a lengthy speech about all the good work that Lina had done over the years for the less fortunate in the community. Harry, who hadn't known about Lina's volunteer work, listened intently. Afterwards, others spoke, friends and neighbors and relatives who had specific recollections they wanted to share, but Harry only half listened to them because he could see that things were winding down and he had yet to locate Iris's face in the crowd. Finally he spotted her, standing arm in arm with a short, heavy-set man not far behind the neighbor women, Carol and Pat. He intended to approach her immediately after the service, to find out what, exactly, Lina had left for him and where he could pick it up.

The woman in the striped suit, who had stopped crying and now looked very business like, stepped forward to ask if there was anyone else who wanted to say anything before the group departed for her house for a catered lunch. Iris hadn't said anything about a lunch over the phone, and Harry wondered whether this was an oversight or whether he simply wasn't invited. The idea of attending was intimidating, but on the other hand, he felt he had a right to be there, being the man whom Lina had loved. He bent his head and pondered the possibility of inviting himself, of asking Iris for a ride to the zebra woman's house. But by the time he got done stringing together the words that he would use, in the event that he mustered the courage, the crowd had already thinned substantially and he realized he had lost sight of Iris.

Harry panicked. He lifted his chin and looked in every direction. He hadn't even bothered to note what color dress Iris was wearing, and now with all the black umbrellas receding toward the line of cars, her dress color was the only thing that might have provided a clue. "Shit," he mumbled, and when he noticed the heavy-set man driving off with a passenger in his car, he slapped his palm over his eyes. Now he would have to call Fred and hope he still had Iris's number and would oblige him by giving it out, and then call Iris and find out whom exactly he should contact...and all for what was almost definitely nothing but a box of magazine clippings. It was all so complicated, this, life, everything; it made him long for a drink.

Harry let his hand slip from his face and found himself looking at Lina's grave stone. He hadn't been able to see it before, because of the crowd. Even at this distance he could see that there were two names on it. He moved in its direction, slowly, heavily, as if against the weight of his sudden despondency. He couldn't think why he should feel so overwhelmed at the sight of Lina's husband's name on the stone. After all, it wasn't as if he hadn't know that she had been married. There had been a moment during the service when Harry had experienced an urge to raise his hand, to catch the zebra woman's eye and declare that he too had something to say about Lina. Now he was glad he hadn't.

"Are you Harry Rawley?" a woman's voice cried out.

Harry turned and found himself looking at the woman in the striped suit. Again he was struck by her familiarity, but he was too flabbergasted by her sudden appearance to mention it. He nodded.

"Lina told me about you," Trish said. "I'd expected to meet you in the hospital, but I guess you couldn't make it." She hesitated, as if she thought he should make some response to that. "Did Iris tell you that Lina left you something?"

Harry looked at the stone, then back at the woman. He managed another nod.

Trish sighed. Then she straightened and that business-like look came over her again. "She wanted you to have her car," she said sharply and with resolve.

Harry could only stare at her. He thought about the way the engine rattled, and the strange smell it had emitted whenever Lina had accelerated. The car would cost more to fix up than he had. Then all at once he remembered that Lina had professed to love the car, for sentimental reasons, she'd said. She'd said that the last time he'd seen her. His face lit up, but Trish, who was busy fumbling in her bag, didn't notice.

"You should be very pleased," she went on. "It's a beauty and Lina took very good care of it. You know she bought it back when—"

Harry coughed a laugh. "A beauty?" he interrupted.

Trish looked up abruptly, her hand still in her bag but motionless now. Gradually, she turned her head to look over her shoulder, at the few cars that remained in the cemetery. When she turned back to him, she was grinning. And Harry, who believed his bad manners responsible for her amusement, blushed.

Trish's hand went back to work, more slowly now, and in a

moment she produced a piece of paper and a pen. She wrote her number on it and handed it to him. "Well, it was a beauty in Lina's eyes," she said. "There's just no accounting for some people's tastes." She stopped to smile and shake her head. "You give me another week or so and then give me a call and I'll make arrangements to get the Chevy over to you."

Harry shook his head. "No, no. I'll find a way to come and get it. Don't put yourself to no bother on my account."

Her fingertips alighted on his hand, immediately silencing him. "Don't be silly. It won't be any bother at all," she declared cheerfully, and she flashed him a smile as she turned to go.

Harry went away smiling too. And some moments later, when he stopped short and turned around, having just realized where he had seen the zebra woman before (she was the one in the picture with Lina on the dresser), he was surprised to note the distance that she had covered in so short a time. Why, if he had stopped but a moment later, she would have gotten into the Caddy she was heading for and he would have missed his chance. "Miss!" he called out.

Trish stopped in her tracks, and it took so long for her to turn around and acknowledge him that for a moment Harry thought that he must have blundered again, by shouting like that in a cemetery. He lifted his arm, "I just wanted to thank you, Miss Plath," he yelled.

She raised her own arm then and waved heartily in recognition of his gratitude.

ME AND BOBBY DENIRO

OUT IN FRONT OF THE BABALAND

I SLIP THE INDIGO GIRLS INTO THE CD player attached to my dash. As I crank up the volume and begin to sing along, I glance in the rearview—at my eyes, brows, and forehead—and decide that at forty-six I am still beautiful. It is the lower part of my face, the part I cannot see in the rearview, that gives my age away, but I'm not inclined to think about that at the moment. It is a beautiful November day, and I am on my way to Robert DeNiro's house.

Finding out Robert DeNiro's address was no easy task. All I had to go on was an article that appeared in the local newspaper saying that there was a rumor afloat that he'd purchased a 6,000 square foot mansion on 100 acres with a half-mile of river frontage up here in the Hudson Valley. The article said the rumor could not be confirmed, that the county realtors were tight-lipped on the subject (hard to imagine, that), and that the county clerk had a record of a deed transfer of a house meeting the aforementioned description, but that it was from an individual to a trust and that neither of the trustees' names was DeNiro.

Luckily, I happen to know some not-so-tight-lipped realtors, and a few people in the appraisal business as well. And after a long afternoon spent on the phone, I found myself talking to the secretary whose boss had done the appraisal. I told her I was considering having my home appraised and wondered if the estimate of value would be affected by the proximity of the DeNiro property. When she asked me where I lived, so that she could make that determination, I made something up. "How close is that to Palmer Road?" she asked in response, and thus I had my answer. I took out a road map, ascertained that Palmer could be reached via Weston Ave, which meets it in the middle.

I went out there yesterday, to check things out. When I got to the "T" I turned right and drove for several miles without seeing anything that approached the newspaper description of the house. No, in fact, the houses I passed were all rather shabby, a lot of them, like a good many places out this way, having an abundance of outbuildings surrounding them, sheds to shelter sheep and goats and firewood. I turned around and went back the other way, passing Weston and driving several miles more. The houses there suggested a bit more affluence, but I still didn't see anything that looked like it could be the DeNiro property. These homes were all new, some of them a bit gaudy in my opinion with their turrets and second-floor balconies, and the DeNiro house was supposed to be over 200 years old. I was thinking that I gone through all this trouble for nothing when I turned a bend and there it was, the last house on the road. I'd expected it to be at some distance from the road, but it was right there in front of me, looming over me almost, a huge, old, stately mansion surrounded by a high, wrought-iron fence. It had to be the place.

I didn't linger. There was something threatening about the house—its unexpected proximity perhaps, or perhaps it was the fence, the vertical shafts of which came to a point at the top so that they resembled a line of javelins. In any case, there was an inviolability about the place that made me feel the way I do when I find myself driving on a narrow road between two rock cuts. I made a U-turn and hit the gas.

Back at home, I spent the next few hours sitting before the computer in the spare bedroom composing the letter, or rather composing several letters, each varying in style but all alike in content. When I finally came up with one that satisfied me, I went into the living room, where Patrick (Trick, I call him) was reading the newspaper. I'm quite good at letter writing, and I wanted him to hear this one. Besides being well-written, it was amusing, and, I felt, highly persuasive. "Do you want me to read you the letter I've written to Robert DeNiro?" I asked. He lowered the paper, revealing the two dark weapons, gun barrels they look like, which are his eyes. "No," was all he said. Then he disappeared behind his paper again.

I went back into the spare room then and called Lacy, my best friend, and read her the letter. She agreed with me that it was well written and amusing, but then Lacy would say that anyway because she likes me an awful lot, and her own marriage being so secure and her heart being the size that it is, she has been overly considerate of my feelings these last few months. When we were done discussing the merits of my letter, I whined for a while about Trick's reaction when I'd offered to read it to him. "He didn't even ask me why I was writing to Robert DeNiro," I said, my voice so nasal I might have been holding my nose. "He isn't the least bit curious about what I do or why I do it."

You may be wondering yourself why I wrote Robert DeNiro a letter. Do you remember a poem by Edwin Arlington Robinson called "The Mill"? About a woman fretting over the fact that her husband has not yet come home and recalling that the last thing he said before he left in the morning was, "There are no millers any more"? And then she goes out to the mill where he used to work, and sure enough, he's hung himself? Well, I'm not a miller, but my occupational prospects have likewise dried up. And while I'd never consider hanging myself, I do understand why the miller did.

You see, back before my boys were born, I used to design book covers. I worked for Simon and Schuster, commuted into Manhattan each day and sat drawing in my own little cubicle. My boss's secretary brought me coffee in the mornings, a menu from wherever she and the boss were ordering in from for lunch, and what was at that time considered a hefty paycheck at the end of each week. But I quit just before the boys' births (virtually simultaneous since they're twins), figuring I could pick up some freelance work once they started school, that in the meantime I'd finally have an opportunity to concentrate on my oil painting. (I had sold two paintings by that time, one of them for $900.)

The problem was that my boys were a handful, even after school began. Terry was a magnet for bacteria, and if I wasn't bringing him to the doctor, I was sitting at his bedside reading him Richard Scarry books and pouring aspirins down his throat. Wally didn't get sick nearly as often, but he required just as much time and energy, for his ambition was (isn't anymore, thank God) to be a stand-up comedian, and of course he practiced his comedy routines in the classroom while his various teachers were working hard at their own deliveries. The result was that I spent as much time consulting with his teachers as I did with Terry's doctors.

And both boys were very active. Terry was musically inclined but couldn't decide which instrument he favored, so naturally we tried them all. Finally, in junior high, he settled on the stand-up bass, which meant I could no longer impose on any of his fellow musicians' mothers to drive him to lessons and performances when I had scheduling conflicts. No, in fact, I finally had to buy a pick-up truck with a cap just so I could haul his bass around easily, because before that I had a Toyota, a Celica, and Terry and I would be outside in the driveway screaming at each other while we tried to cram his bass into the back seat, and then Terry would have to sit with his head at an angle to allow room for the instrument's protruding neck. And Wally was a jock, and his fellow jocks apparently didn't even have mothers, for somehow I found myself in the unenviable position of driving all of them to baseball, basketball, and soccer practices and games all the time.

The years passed, and by the time Terry's immune system kicked in and Wally decided there was more security in law than in stand-up comedy, by the time they were both able to drive themselves to their sundry activities, the graphic art industry had become all but entirely computerized. I got a computer of course, charged it along with some software that I'm still paying interest on, but no matter how aesthetically pleasing my resume may be (I'm a genius at matching up congenial fonts), there's no way to hide the fact that I am merely a homemaker whose graphic art experience took place in what might as well be another lifetime. Oh, sure, I get a freelance assignment now and then, usually from some small, local company verging on bankruptcy and therefore appreciative of the fact that my rates are half of those of anyone else. And I've sold three more oil paintings too, though none for more than $500. But the truth is that I couldn't live a year on what I've made in the last ten. Of course Trick makes enough money to support us, but it's just enough, especially now that the boys are in college, and as he reminds me at least twice daily, it'd be nice to have a little extra.

Unlike me, Trick has always been attuned to current trends. He owned and managed a frame shop for a while, but back in the early eighties when property prices were at an all-time low, he sold the business to one of his employees and used the proceeds to buy a small, dilapidated office building down in Centertown. He drove an oil truck in the meantime, so that he could pay the bills without having to dip into any of the money he'd set aside to refurbish his acquisition. Then, in the late eighties, when the building was in tip-top shape and the office space was all rented out, he sold it, for four times the amount he'd paid for it. His profits sat in the bank up until '91. Then, one fateful night in the middle of the winter, he plopped himself down on the sofa in our family room and said, "What do the babyboomers need most?" "Hormones?" I ventured, for even before Crystal, our sex life had begun to decline. He paid no attention to me, hadn't been talking to me in the first place. Benson was over, our friend then and Trick's partner now. "Something to do with aging?" Benson asked. Trick sat forward and flung a finger into the air to let him know that he was on the right track. "And what happens to people when they age?" "They get stupid," giggled Millie, Benson's wife, who was on the kitchen side of the snack bar with me guzzling down her second glass of wine and thus getting a little stupid herself. "They get sick?" Benson queried. "Exactly!" Trick cried. "And when they do, they need walkers, hospital beds, wheelchairs, oxygen tanks…"

So now Trick and Benson are the proud owners of a hospital equipment and supply store. But our friendship with Millie and Benson suffered for it, because of course Trick didn't feel like socializing on weekends with someone he had to look at all day. And then it died altogether this past summer, because Millie was the one who finally got sick and tired of hearing me complain about Trick's behavior and informed me that there was a reason for it and that Crystal was its name—which naturally ticked off Trick no end.

But I've digressed.

My therapist once told me this story about two monks that belonged to a sect that was not allowed to touch women—I mean, not even to shake hands. And one day they're walking along and they see a woman trying to get across a raging stream, and Monk Number One goes right up to her and lifts her in his arms and carries her across and puts her down on the other side and then returns to his side of the bank. The monks continue their walk in silence, and after they've put several miles behind them, Monk Number One asks Monk Number Two why he's so quiet. Monk Number Two says, "You know we're not supposed to touch women," and Monk Number One replies, "I put her down hours ago. You're still carrying her."

So, anyway, I got to thinking recently that finding work, bringing in more than a few dollars here and there with the freelancing and the oil painting, would both distract me and please Trick. But I didn't want to look for a full-time job, because then I wouldn't be able to paint at all, and in spite of the fact that I'm running out of time, that I have friends my age who are easing toward retirement, I can't seem to rid myself of the notion (some forty years in the making now) that I will one day be a successful artist. I started looking for part-time work therefore, but everyone I called either wanted skills I didn't have, or wasn't prepared to pay me enough money to make working out (what, with clothes and gas) practical, or was offering a position so prosaic that my beagle Timothy could have filled it. I mean, this is not Manhattan; this area is not exactly a mecca for stimulating business activity. Then, when I saw the DeNiro article, I got to thinking that if he's going to be coming up here on weekends, which I imagine is his intention, he's going to be needing someone to open up his house for him, you know, give it a good cleaning, throw a couple of logs on the grate, put some flowers on the dining room table, and stock some necessities in the fridge so that he doesn't have to subject himself to long lines and opportunistic windbags at Shop Rite. So I wrote him the letter, told him I could handle all that for him, that I was prepared to do whatever he required to make his recreation time just that, and that if he had some need that went beyond my province—rewiring or roof-tile replacement for instance—that I, having lived here all these years, was in a much better position to obtain fair estimates than he, and that furthermore I could make myself available to oversee the work when the time came to carry it out.

I exaggerated a bit, implying that I did this sort of thing professionally. But then again, what woman hasn't done her share of it? Besides, I felt I needed an edge, something to set me apart from any other hungry homemakers who might have the very same thing in mind. But pride motivated me to mention the fact that I'm an artist as well. I didn't want him to get the wrong idea.

I turn the volume down on the Indigo Girls as I round the bend. Even though I have been here before, seeing the house so close so suddenly unnerves me all over again. I feel like a trespasser, which, I suppose, I am. There are no cars in the driveway, but then there wouldn't be, would there? The rumor is that Mr. DeNiro already has a pad out back, for the helicopter that will be transporting him to and from his new home. If he has a car here, it would be in the garage, so that people like me won't know whether he's in or not. Since he has only just purchased the house, I don't imagine he's done much more than come by to measure the rooms yet. I mean, he'll need furniture and appliances and kitchen utensils and linens before he actually moves in.

I pull up beside the mailbox, and leaving the truck running, I open the door and jump out with the letter. I pull down the mailbox latch and am shocked to see that the box is full of mail. It occurs to me that some mechanical device may be taking my picture. I tip my head, so that my hair falls in my face. Then I slide my letter onto the top of the pile and jump back into the truck. I make a U-turn and take off down the road.

On the way home I have second thoughts about what I've done. I become so preoccupied with them that I don't even think to turn the CD volume back up. As I am checking the rearview to see whether someone is following me (DeNiro's security people?), I lift my head a bit too high and consequently glimpse my jaw line and remember my age. I feel a bit foolish. I decide not to tell anyone who doesn't already know about what I have done.

Trick is a man of order. He likes his dinner on the table at the same time each evening. And although it is now approaching the hour when I should be in the kitchen preparing it, I decide to take a detour and go to Pine Street, where all my favorite shops are located, and look in the windows at the things that I will be able to buy once I start cleaning Mr. DeNiro's house. I don't want to take advantage of the fact that he's a millionaire by charging him an arm and a leg, but I figure he's used to paying city wages for such services, and because of the size of the house, a few hundred bucks for a day's work will not be out of line—especially if he wants the logs and the flowers and the other amenities.

I have always felt guilty about spending money on myself, but the prospect of finally making some inspires me to enter the shoe store. This is one of those expensive shops that sells European merchandise exclusively. Unlike American manufacturers, the Europeans seem to understand that comfort is as important as style when it comes to women's footwear. My eye falls on a pair of black leather boots that look like the kind that my sons' girlfriends wear. I look inside and ascertain that they were made in Holland. The leather is incredibly soft, and I like the square toe and the fat, two-inch heel. The boys' college educations are taking a toll, Trick says on those rare occasions when he sees me come in with a bag which is not from the grocery store. Why do I need clothes anyway, he asks, when I seldom leave the house? If I worked, he says, he could see the point.

Since the summer, since Crystal, I have been on my best behavior, my thinking being that if he strayed once, he could easily stray again. Crystal, he says when I force him to talk about it, was my fault. If I'd shown him more respect…if I hadn't always put the boys first…

But having just come from putting a letter in Robert DeNiro's mailbox makes me feel a bit insolent (the feeling of foolishness is hovering just below the surface now), and I decide that in spite of what Trick may or may not say, I must have the boots. Thinking that I can make casseroles all week with leftovers from the freezer, I use my grocery money to pay for them. And when I realize that I still have twenty dollars left, I put half of it down on a beautiful black leather shoulder bag that I can pay off after my first day at the DeNiro house.

When I pull into the driveway, I see that Trick is already home. If I walk in with the bag from the shoe store, there will be two strikes against me instead of only the one having to do with the dinner delay. But there is nowhere to hide the bag in the little cab of my truck, and the back of the truck is out of the question because I've taken the cap off. Trick likes to go out in the evenings; once a week he plays racquetball, and at least twice a week he returns to the store after dinner to work on the books and see to other tasks that he cannot seem to get to during business hours. Since my truck is parked right beside his Audi, he need only glance in its direction to observe a bag sitting on the seat or the floor. Hoping that he is not watching from the window, I get out with the bag, then lift the lid on the trash can as I pass it, and deposit my precious purchase within. Then I open the door, and stepping over Timothy, who has run to the door to greet me, I go right into the kitchen and turn on the oven. I hear movement in the living room, the rustle of paper and the whoosh of the sofa as it gives up Trick's weight. I promise myself that I will not tell him that I placed a letter in Robert DeNiro's mailbox. He would only laugh at me. It would only give him an excuse to lecture me about going out and getting a real job. Like a mantra, I repeat this promise over and over in my mind, because the fact of the matter is that I am still too keyed up, and in spite of the fact that I know his reaction would be disapproving, I find I want very much to tell someone. I feel like a kid who has just stolen a candy bar from the drug store. I want someone to snicker with me, to pat me on the back and applaud my chutzpah. I turn from the refrigerator with a pan of enchiladas left over from last night's dinner and bend to put it into the oven. I am still wearing my gloves and jacket. "Busy afternoon?" Trick queries as he appears on the other side of the snack counter.

I straighten and look at him. His head is tipped down. He is looking at me over his glasses. The muscles around his mouth are entirely slack. "Remember that letter I told you I wrote?" I say. I am shocked at my lack of control and wonder if it constitutes some mild form of Tourette's. "Well, I put it in his mailbox…DeNiro's."

His face becomes animated so suddenly it makes me wince. "You put a letter into Robert DeNiro's mailbox?" he says loudly, laughing. Then, just as suddenly, he is sober again. "That's a federal offense."

"People do it all the time," I reply, turning back to the refrigerator. I try to sound casual, but the truth is that the illegality of my deed had not occurred to me before. I remove a container of rice left over from Chinese take-out some nights ago. "Why, just last week someone with a plowing service stuck a flyer in our box. Remember?"

He shakes his head. "You're not allowed to do that either. But a sealed letter without a stamp, if that's what you did…that's tampering with the mail. If he decides to press charges—"

I remember again the panic I experienced when I opened the mailbox and found it full. "He wouldn't do that. He's not that kind of person," I interrupt.

"How do you know what kind of person he is?"

I shrug indifferently, but I am already imagining headlines: SCORNED WOMAN ARRESTED FOR TAMPERING WITH ROBERT DENIRO'S MAIL. "So," he says, lifting the rice container, looking, no doubt, for an expiration date, "are you going to tell me what the letter said or not?"

"I thought he might need some help," I reply indignantly. "Someone to clean his house, that sort of thing."

He turns his head from side to side, stopping to let his gaze rest on the portion of the counter on which I let mail and receipts and other miscellaneous documents accumulate. You don't clean this house, he is thinking, but he only says, "I'm going upstairs to take a nap. Call me when dinner's ready." I watch him retreat, then listen to the sound of his footsteps on the stairs. When I hear the bedroom door close behind him, I run outside and retrieve my new boots from the trash can.

I do not expect to hear from Robert DeNiro until the weekend, but just in case I clear my throat each time the phone rings and answer in a voice that is not unlike Kathleen Turner's. Then on Friday, while I am in the basement working on a painting, Trick plays a little joke on me. He calls from the store, and when I answer, he says, "Rita? Bobby here." He holds something over the phone, a handkerchief perhaps, so that his voice is muffled, and in the solitary second that it takes before I realize it is not Robert DeNiro on the other end of the line, my heart leaps into my throat and I look to see what I am wearing. Then I realize that it is Trick and scream at him for trying to make a fool of me. "You have no sense of humor, Rita," he says when I pause to catch my breath. "Never did. That's one of our problems."

I take his declaration back down to the basement with me. The cow on my canvas, with her long face and insipid stare, seems to confirm his remark. Suddenly I don't feel like working on her anymore. I look at the paintings leaning against the wall beyond my easel. Most of them are rural scenes—mountains, rivers, creeks, wildflowers, deer, barns, cottages in the woods. Some of them represent their subjects so well they could pass for photographs. I lack imagination, I decide.

I clean my brushes and go upstairs to lie down on the sofa. My life feels overwhelmingly empty just now, and I chalk that fact up to Trick's indifference. We have friends who don't feel the need to share the same bedroom anymore. Trick and I still do—as far as I know. Ever since Crystal, Trick comes to bed late, well after I'm asleep, and rises early, before I get up, so I never actually see him in bed beside me. His side of the bed is always mussed in the morning, but for all I know he sneaks up, rumples the blankets and pillow, and goes back down to sleep on the sofa.

Suddenly I have an idea. I leap up from the sofa so fast it makes me dizzy and run into the kitchen to snatch a piece of paper toweling from the roll. Then I pick up the phone and place the paper towel over the mouthpiece and dial Trick's shop. When he answers, I speak in a voice a few octaves higher than my own, the kind I imagine would be appropriate for a twenty-five-year-old. "Pat?" I ask, and when he affirms, I say, "It's Crystal. How are you?"

It is quiet for a moment. Then, in a voice so low it could be called a growl, Trick says, "You think that's funny?"

"Oh, come on," I cry, balling up the paper towel and tossing it into the trash can. "It was just a joke. Where's your sense of humor?"

Later, I get to thinking that if it had been Robert DeNiro on the phone, and if he had wanted me to come right over for an interview, I wouldn't have been able to find a thing in my closet appropriate to wear. I mean, of course I will wear old jeans and flannel shirts when I actually go to clean, but an interview, even if it's for a house-cleaning position, should be a dignified affair. I would like to be able to wear my new boots when I go—but with what?

I find myself back on Pine Street, this time armed with a credit card that we received in the mail a few months ago and put aside for emergencies. The bill won't come for a month, I figure, and by that time I will be gainfully employed and able to pay for my purchases myself.

As I am looking through the racks in the Pine Street Boutique, a memory from years ago, from back when Trick and I were first dating, surfaces. Trick and I were out in front of a movie theater, a little early for the film we'd come to see. I was wearing a short, tight-fitting denim skirt and a bolero-style denim jacket and Trick was in jeans and an off-white cotton sweater. My legs were bare, I recall; I was wearing white sneakers and thick white socks folded at the ankles. On my head I wore a beret, black, it must have been, to match the form-fitting lacy shell I wore beneath the jacket. I'd placed the beret at an angle. My hair was long back then, and lighter and thicker than it is now. It poured out from under my hat like honey, flowing over my shoulders and down my back. We could have been brother and sister, Trick and me—both of us tall, thin, blonde, healthy-looking…beautiful.

We were flirting with each other, I recall. This was back in the days when we couldn't talk to each other without smiling, and we were smiling and teasing and joking and laughing, standing out there in front of the movie theater. I don't remember what we were saying anymore, but I remember our movements as if it were yesterday. Trick had his hands in his pockets, and, as we conversed, he stepped forward, back, to the side, employing a sort of box step to shift his weight around. I had my hands clasped behind my back, and I was stepping back and forth and to the side too, my feet rising behind and before me, little coquettish kicks executed with a slight turning of the hip.

You know what I mean; you've seen young people swaying to the beat of love's drum before.

And while we were engaged in this mating ritual, this emotional shuffle, a car pulled up in front of the theater, which I probably would not have noticed, given my self-absorption, but as it happened, Trick offered me a cigarette just then. I stepped forward, anchored for that instant, so that he could light it for me. And it was then, as I was bending over the flame in his hand, my head tilted so that my hair wouldn't burn, that I happened to notice the car and the look on the face of the driver. He was staring at us, at Trick and me, with a kind of Woody Allen expression—curious and sad and hopeless all at once. The woman beside him, meanwhile, craned her neck to see the signboard on which the times of the movie showings were listed. Then she said something to the man. She looked disgusted, as if she had known all along that the movie they'd wanted to see wouldn't be playing—or maybe wouldn't be starting at the time they'd hoped. Still looking at me and Trick, the man nodded an acknowledgment, which the woman couldn't have seen because she hadn't even turned to him when she'd spoken. Then my cigarette was lit, and the car pulled away, and Trick and I reverted back to our lover's shuffle, swinging our cigarettes at our sides, lifting our heads to the darkening sky so we wouldn't blow smoke in each other's faces. But the look on the man's face stayed with me, because I knew what he had been thinking. Trick and I represented something he had lost, something he regretted losing and knew he would never get back again. And I was just a little bit scared after that.

I take a skirt from the rack and hold it out for a better look. It is the kind of thing I usually wear for social events, long and flowing, small flowers on a dark background. I replace it after a moment and wander over to the corner where the sale items are. DeNiro, it occurs to me, may ask to see my paintings. They'd be perfect in a house like his, a fact which I hinted at in my letter. I pull out a long black skirt from the rack and imagine myself wearing it in DeNiro's unfurnished kitchen. I see myself leaning against the cupboards in it, DeNiro standing across from me, barefoot, holding a coffee mug in one hand, sizing me up, wondering whether it would be wise to bring up the paintings or whether we should stick to domestic affairs.

I wander over to the corner where the younger women's clothes are displayed. All of a sudden a young woman appears beside me, a beautiful young woman; she could be Crystal for all I know. I never met Crystal myself, but once, when Trick was feeling particularly melancholy, I got him to describe her for me. Long limbs, he said, long hair, full lips, turned-up nose, small, firm breasts like apples. ("Well, you asked," he snapped when I started to cry.)

The young woman beside me chooses a pair of black leather pants from the rack and a short wheat-colored cotton turtleneck from the shelf above it. She goes into the dressing room, and a moment later she comes out to look at herself in the mirrors that line one wall. The two young salesgirls descend on her, telling her how great she looks. She shakes her head. Not quite what she was looking for, she says. Her breasts are large, I notice, more like melons than apples. Now that I know that she is not Crystal, I can go back to looking for something for myself.

I leave the store an hour later with my head up, indignant because I imagine that the salesgirls will begin to giggle as soon as the door closes behind me. I resist the temptation to look back through the glass to see whether I am right. I am fragile these days; I am learning to protect myself.

Once I am home, I carefully separate my new acquisitions from the lengths of purple tissue in which they were wrapped. I lay them out on my bed then glance at the clock. There is still time to try them on before Trick gets home.

Shame on me. The pants are leather, black, slick-looking, and incredibly soft. The turtleneck is wheat-colored. Yes, of course; it is the very same outfit that the girl who might have been Crystal tried on, only two or three sizes larger. I never tried it on in the store. I don't even know if it will fit.

I retrieve a pair of black stockings from the drawer and then dig my new boots out from their hiding place in the back of the closet. I throw off my clothes, my jeans and sweatshirt, and slip into the new things. Then I stand before the mirror for a full five minutes considering. The pants are too tight around my stomach. It makes my little paunch look even bigger than it really is. The shirt, being form-fitting, isn't any help. But from my hips down and my midriff up, I look just fine.

All I need, I decide, is a vest, something to cover the middle area.

By Saturday I am all ready for Robert DeNiro's phone call. Trick is at work. The new vest, which consists of colorful silk patch-work squares hand-stitched onto a black rayon background, is hanging in the back of my closet, behind the summer clothes. The box containing the boots is over in the corner of the closet beneath a box containing my summer sandals. The leather bag, which I finally took off of layaway, is back there too. My hair, which I blew-dry on low using a curling brush, looks great.

I sit on the edge of the sofa while I wait, watching one of the two films that I picked up on my way back from Pine Street Video the day before. It is called *The Fan*. I've seen it before, but now that I'm going to be working for the man, I thought it might be a good idea to see it again. The other one is *The Deerslayer*, which I've also seen, twice. I've never seen DeNiro on a talk show. I have no idea what he's really like. My friend Jane told me that he tried to pick up her older sister at a county fair in Ohio in 1965, that her sister said he was dull and had an attitude. Lacy, who has seen him on talk shows, says he's exceedingly intelligent. Lacy says he likes his women black.

I imagine working at his house, cleaning the oven and making the beds while he's off on a shoot. I imagine that he will keep a voice-activated tape recorder hidden somewhere, so that he will know what goes on when he isn't around. I imagine him coming home after I've gone and rewinding the tape. I imagine him smiling when he hears me singing my way through my work.

I serve Trick Pasta e Fagioli in the evening, easy to make and not at all costly since I already had the beans and tomatoes in the pantry. The only thing I had to buy was the macaroni. When he gets up from the table to see what Timothy is barking about in the living room (a car making a U-turn in our driveway, no doubt), I run into the kitchen with his plate and add another ladle full of pasta to it. I am hoping to fill him up so that he won't get hungry later and go rooting around in the refrigerator, which is bare if you don't count the things that are no longer edible. I have to be careful with money now. So far I have spent over $600 on my interview outfit, and I am thinking that my bulky down jacket will look ridiculous with it, that really I should go out and get a new one.

"You know," Trick says later, as I am clearing, "if you really want to clean houses, you should go to an agency. They send you all over, five days a week."

"What!" I nearly drop the plates I am carrying to the sink.

Trick drapes his arm over the back of his chair. He'll stay like that now, talking about whatever and watching me move from the dining room to the kitchen and back again, until his coffee is served. It is virtually the only time we converse. "An agency. A cleaning service," he reiterates. Amazingly enough, his face is completely devoid of humor.

"What can you be talking about?"

"Well, you contacted DeNiro about cleaning, so if you're willing to clean his house, then I assume you're thinking of making a career of it. And frankly, I don't think it's such a bad idea. The guy who owns the coffee shop where I go for lunch? His wife cleans for a living. Makes good money too."

I take a deep breath before I answer. I can see that he's in the mood for a fight, and I don't intend to give him one. Still, I find myself talking through my teeth. "I contacted DeNiro because his house is very large and cleaning it would probably pay well. I did not contact him because I am hoping to make a career out of house-cleaning."

Trick begins to laugh, a bully snicker that makes me think he must have had a lot of enemies when he was a kid. "You know, Rita, at first I thought that this DeNiro thing was about you having a mid-life crisis. But now I see that what it's about is your damn painting! You've rearranged your whole life so that you can go down into the basement and paint cows! Now, I've been telling you that we could use a little more money, and instead of going out and finding a job like anyone else would, you come up with some hair-brain scheme that you imagine will enable you to make a few fast bucks in a few days so you can head right back down into the basement again. Only problem is, in the meantime, I'm working my ass off, putting in six days a week plus some evenings. My tools are down in the basement, Rita. Don't you think I'd like to go down there and play with them every once in a while? But I can't, can I? Because I have to go to work. In fact, I don't even know if we still have a basement. That's how long it's been since I've been down there." He stops to catch his breath. "There still a basement down there, Rita? Is there?"

I squeeze an obscenity out from between my sealed lips, but Trick is too worked up to notice. "Why don't you just give it up, Rita, this idea that one day you're going to be discovered and make a fortune?

177

Why don't you just go out and get a job like everyone else? You're not Walker, you know. It just didn't work out like that for you."

Walker is a friend of ours. He paints for a living. His work hangs in a gallery in Manhattan, and although he only sells an average of one painting every two years, a painting of his will go for six figures, so he gets by.

Later I lie in bed and try to imagine myself putting my painting aside so that I can become a professional housecleaner. My work is good, but compared to Walker's, it is only mediocre. What Trick said is true, I realize. And I hate him as much for knowing the truth as I do for bludgeoning me with it. I will never make money painting. I am self-indulgent. I have taken advantage of the fact that he has supported our family all these years. Now I have become dependent on him—which is not a good thing, because the next time a twenty-five-year-old pays him a little attention, he will leave me.

Trick spends Sunday reading the papers. I spend the day wondering what I will do when DeNiro calls, how I will get out of the house in my new clothes without Trick noticing. I jump every time the phone rings, and as it happens, it rings all day. First Wally calls from his school in Oswego, then Trick's parents call from Ohio, then my father calls from Florida, and then Terry calls from Louisiana State. Trick and I take turns speaking to each of them. Trick talks to everyone about how his business is doing; I talk to them about the weather. By the end of the day I can't remember who was cold and who was staying in because of the rain and who couldn't wait to get out into the sunshine. Then, towards evening, I get a call from Frank Rogers, who is on the Board of Directors at the Babaland, an aging, nonprofit theater in a depressed section of Lumbertown, up on the mountain, about fifteen miles from where I live.

This is a surprise. During the spring I do a lot of volunteer work for the Babaland, mostly advising them about the sets for the theater productions they put on in July and August. But the Babaland is closed this time of year, to save on utilities.

Frank, a long-time devotee of the arts, is so excited that he jumbles his words and has to start over. What's happened is that James Field, who owns the Lumbertown Bank, has donated a large sum of money to the Babaland, and consequently they're planning some winter events for the first time ever. The first one is to be a poetry reading/performance, right after the first of the year. The theme of the reading will be the conflict between the spirit's craving for concord and the realities of living in the technological age. Frank informs me that the board has decided that it would be appropriate to hang artwork in the lobby the night of the show, half of it depicting nature and the other half computer-generated illustrations featuring such subjects as suited figures carrying attaches and walking on surfaces covered with currency. He wants me not only to contribute some of my paintings for the event, but also to head the committee in charge of acquiring rural works from other local artists.

On Monday, I give DeNiro about three hours, and when he doesn't call, I drive up the mountain to the Babaland to meet with George Brewer, the Babaland's Artistic Director—or the Baba King, as some of us call him behind his back. George is a nice man, after he's had five or six beers, and the rest of the time he's a tyrant. But the truth of the matter is that he gets things done. Everyone hustles when George is around. You'd never know that his laborers were all volunteers.

I knock on his office door and wait. At first I think that no one is there, but after about five minutes, George calls for me to come in. I find him sitting at his desk with his back to me, creating what seems to be an invitation for the poetry event on his computer. He is fooling around with fonts at the moment, trying to find the right one to set the time and date text in. I sigh loudly, but he doesn't turn around until he has finally chosen a font. And then he doesn't smile. "Frank got hold of you?" he asks.

I am tempted to say, No, I'm here because I like you, Ratface. But instead I mumble, "Yes, he called last night."

"And he told you we want you to head the rural art committee?"

"Yes. I've made a list of the artists I thought we should contact."

I take the list out of my bag and hold it out to him. He snatches it, then covers his bottom lip with his finger and reads it carefully. Then he swivels back to his desk and scribbles something, one long, thin, denim-clad leg remaining out at an angle like an anchor. When he returns the list to me, three of the names I'd come up with are scratched off and two more have been added. "That's it," he says, and until he swivels back to his desk a moment later, I don't know whether he means that's the list, as in 'and there won't be any further alterations to it,' or 'that's it, you're dismissed.'

How is it possible, I wonder, that I have put aside my painting time to drive fifteen miles to hand George Brewer a list I could have discussed with him over the phone? Why do all the men I know treat me the same way? I am about to leave when George, who is back at work on his computer again, speaks. "We're sending out over three-hundred invitations. We're going to need some people to print out the labels, stick them on the invitations, and seal the invitations shut. Can I count on you?"

"Sure. Why not."

"Thursday night then. Here."

I turn to go, but something occurs to me. "You know, George, Bobby DeNiro just bought a place in the neighborhood. You should add his name to the mailing list. He might be interested in attending the event…now that he's part of the community."

George's hands freeze over the keyboard, then drop to his lap. He turns around slowly and stares at me. Initially, I stare back at him. I think it is the first time I've ever looked him full in the face. He reminds me of the early Beatles—any one of them—with his mop of thick brown hair and his boyish face. His teeth are funny. Some of them overlap. I can't think what could be so astonishing about my remark that he should stare at me like this. He looks amused, or at least on the verge of being amused. He looks like Trick does when he knows he is leading me somewhere from which I will momentarily make a fool of myself. I wonder if it's possible that he knows I've gone and put a housecleaning solicitation letter in Robert DeNiro's mailbox. Or maybe it's just the Bobby that got him.

The moment drags on; I look at my hands, his computer, the floor, the calendar on the wall—anything that might hasten it along. But still he continues to stare at me. I can feel my face reddening, my heart pounding. Why don't I just turn and go? I wonder. Then all at once Susie, George's right-hand woman, comes flying in from the adjoining office. "Rita!" she cries when she sees me. "I didn't know you were here? Isn't this exciting? An event in January?"

"Yes," I say, and I sigh with relief when I see from the corner of my eye that George has swiveled back to face his computer.

Susie has a list in her hands. She waves it at me. "Forty-four names we're adding to our mailing list," she boasts. "All contacts

George here has made since our summer season ended. I told him we should call Robert DeNiro, see whether he'd like his name added to our list now that he owns a home in the area. You hear about that?"

I laugh abruptly, and far too loud. "I just said the very same thing to George. And he looked at me like I was crazy."

"George is crazy," Susie exclaims. I feel my brows arch up in horror, but George does not react. I wonder if he and Susie are having an affair. "He doesn't think DeNiro would lower himself to come to one of our events," Susie continues. "But you know what? I'm going to go ahead and add his name anyway. I'm not even going to call him. Only problem is, I don't know his address."

They are, I decide; Susie and the Baba King are sleeping together. It's all I can do to keep from shaking my head and clicking my tongue. I am amused right up until I remember that I sleep with no one. "I'll make a few calls," I promise, "see if I can get an address from one of my realtor friends."

I stop at Pine Street yet one more time. I had given up the notion of buying a new jacket because of the expense, but now I'm not so sure that's a good idea. I mean, it doesn't matter what kind of outerwear I wear to the interview, because I can slip it off as soon as I'm in the door and before Mr. DeNiro has a chance to notice how the pockets had to be stitched back in place on my old parka. But I'll need something nice to wear for the poetry reading, the showing of my art.

I know what I'm buying even before I walk into the Pine Street Boutique. It is there in the new window display, currently being worn by a headless, hipless mannequin. She has her hand in the back pocket of her jeans, so that the jacket, which is open, is pulled back to reveal the snazzy sweater she wears beneath it. She's wearing more necklaces than I would ever wear with such a casual outfit. The jacket is beautiful though, a big, roomy, bomber-style black leather jacket.

The poetry reading/art show is almost two months away. I figure by the time it comes, I will already have been in and out of DeNiro's house, albeit with mops and buckets, several times. Chances are that I will be given a key, that except for the initial interview, we will never be in the house together at the same time. But we will still have plenty of opportunities to communicate.

Since I will be the one emptying his trash cans, if he throws out the Babaland invitation, I will simply retrieve it, tuck a corner of it under the vase of flowers I plan to put on his dining room table whether he requests it or not. Beside it I will leave a note telling him that my paintings will be among those hanging in the lobby that night, that, more importantly, his presence would mean so much to our little rural community, that the Babaland has seen better days, but that he has the power to change that—because of course if the rumor gets around that he came to one event, people will show up in droves for the next one.

I hide my new leather jacket in the back of the closet with the rest of the stuff, and when Trick comes home, I ask him whether or not he plans to attend the Babaland event, which I told him about last night after Frank's phone call. His lip curls immediately. "What, I have to tell you now! It's two months away, Rita."

I ask only to needle him; there is no doubt in my mind that he will come. While he has never been drawn to poetry, he is fiercely drawn to any kind of gathering at which the more affluent members of our community may be in attendance. And as it happens, a good number of the more affluent members of our community are Babaland patrons.

But Trick will not arrive on time; I know that just as surely as I know that he will come. He will calculate the most likely time for an intermission and arrive then, while everyone is mulling about in the lobby. He will shake some hands, answer some questions regarding his business activities, and dolefully follow the crowds back into the theater for the second part of the show. Afterwards, he will be one of the last to leave.

Trick turns off the television at about ten and asks whether we have any wine in the house. Since we never drink unless we have company, and since Trick never turns off the television while I am in his presence, I am momentarily stunned and cannot think of a suitable answer. When my mind starts working again, I see through its eye the bottle of champagne on the bottom shelf of the refrigerator, the one that has been rolling back and forth for a year now in reaction to the leftovers I occasionally slide in beside it. "We have champagne," I say.

"Why don't you open it? I'm in the mood for a drink."

I get up obediently and move into the kitchen. Something is happening here, and I'm not sure what it is. I wash the dust out of the champagne glasses. Then I open the bottle.

When I return to the living room, the TV is back on, the same football game that Trick was watching before, only now he's got it on mute. I give him the glass and sit down on the sofa, not beside him, but not too far away either, just in case it turns out that a desire for intimacy has taken hold of him out of the blue. I don't really think that's the case, but I don't plan to dismiss the possibility either.

With his eyes on the screen he says, "So, how you been? It seems like we don't get much of a chance to talk anymore."

"I've been fine," I say.

"Good, good. That's good." He sips his champagne, sets the glass down on the coffee table, and waits for one of the players to kick a field goal before he speaks again. "Anything new?"

I can't think of a thing…until Timothy lumbers in from the kitchen. "I made an appointment to take Timothy to the vet next week," I say, "for shots."

Trick turns to look at me, but his gaze slides back to the TV before I can read his expression. "No, I meant is there anything new in the job department?"

"Well, actually, in fact, I didn't want to say anything to you in case it doesn't work out, but I have two interviews next week."

Trick's brows vault a good inch. He almost smiles. "What kind of jobs?"

"One's desktop publishing for a public relations firm, newsletters, I think, and the other one I don't know much about. The ad just said they were looking for someone artistically inclined."

Now Trick does smile, and I'm pleased with myself. I don't lie often; I never know whether or not I'll be successful.

We finish off the champagne in our glasses in silence, the both of us smiling vaguely and staring at the still-mute screen. Then I go into the kitchen to get the bottle. When I return and Trick looks at me questioningly, I say, "You can't cork champagne. We may as well finish it up."

But his expression doesn't alter, and I realize that he's not even looking at the champagne bottle. He's looking beyond it and me, working something out. "You know, he says once I've sat down and poured, "I don't mean to bug you about this job thing. It must seem like I do, huh?"

"It's okay, Patrick. I understand," I say, and I pat his arm reassuringly.

"It's just that things are tight, with the boys in college and all."

"I realize that. That's why I set up the interviews."

"And you know, Rita, you just never know what's going to happen, when you might find yourself in a position where you have to work. I mean, you have to think about the future. What if I were to die? How long do you think you could live on the life insurance?" He gives his head a shake. "Or even if I get sick. You just don't know. The stories I hear in the shop...you wouldn't believe it. One day everything is fine, and then the next..."

"You're not sick, are you?" I ask considerately.

"No, no, nothing like that. Not that I know of....though I could be and not know it. Or I could be okay today and then tomorrow...."

"Does something hurt?"

"No, I told you—"

"You're just looking out for my future?"

"Yeah, that's it. That's all."

We look at each other for a moment. Then Trick reaches for the remote and turns the volume back up.

There was a time when champagne used to make me silly, but when I go upstairs and get into bed, I realize that what I am is morose. I toss and turn, but I cannot sleep. I cannot imagine a future for myself, and that is clearly a prerequisite for sleep on this particular occasion.

After a while I get up and gently close the bedroom door. Then I turn on the bedside lamp. I remove my nightgown and drape it over the lampshade, so that the light in the room is dusky at best. I open the closet and stare into the dark corner where my new clothes are gathered and waiting. I realize I have attached a significance to them that goes far beyond their function. I return to the bedroom door, press my ear against it until I have confirmed that the game is still on, and then turn the lock.

I move about quietly in the dimly-lit room, efficiently. I open boxes, fumble with hangers, all without making a sound. I imagine that it is the night of the poetry reading, that that is what I am getting dressed for. I imagine that Robert DeNiro and I have planned to meet there, so that he can look at my paintings and also so that we can be together, for, I imagine, we have developed a relationship. How? I ask myself. How would Robert DeNiro have developed a relationship with his cleaning woman? Once I am dressed, I sit down on the edge of the bed to imagine the details in earnest.

Until just recently it has been a purely epistolary relationship, I imagine. I have left little notes for him to see when he comes to the house on the weekends. Did you have any trouble starting the fire? That was the driest wood I could find—that sort of thing. And he has responded in kind: The wood was fine! It went right up! and so on. And then, I imagine, as time went by, I took the initiative and added an element of intimacy to the notes, little pleasantries such as, I hope you have a great weekend and Stay warm; it's supposed to get quite cold—to which, I imagine, he responded in kind.

You get the idea. Notes turn into longer notes. Longer notes turn into letters. And before long I am telling Robert DeNiro all about Trick's indifference, about the decline of my artistic life, about my children, and all sorts of other things that matter to me. And he is telling me all about how lonely it is at the top, how happy it makes him to come into his house after a long week of work and find my letters, confirmation that there are people in the world whose concern for him isn't tied to anything he can do for them—to which I feel compelled to remind him that he is paying me, to which he responds that he is paying me to clean his house, not for the letters, for all the good will, to which I respond that I do have one little request. And it is then, I imagine, that I tell him about the poetry show, remind him about the invitation he received (which, I imagine, I recovered from the trash), explain that my paintings will be there, and that, if he has a chance and isn't too busy, I'd love it if he came—to which he of course responds that he would love to, that he'll meet me there. I offer to buy his ticket, I imagine, and he accepts.

So there we are. I have imagined a prelude for the moment I am about to imagine now.

I get up and stand before the mirror. I imagine that it is dusk—an easy task given the lighting in the room. The mirror, I imagine, is actually the glass facade at the Babaland, and I am standing outside, looking myself over in it. I look great in this light in my new boots, leather pants, and bomber jacket. I have my new shoulder bag flung over my shoulder. My hair is a bit mussed, but then it's a windy evening.

I turn from the glass facade and face the street, where I am momentarily expecting Robert DeNiro to pull up in his chauffeur-driven limo. Besides being windy, it is cold, but I am warm enough in all my leather. As I survey the passing cars, I see the Baba King go by in his old Buick. He drives right past without noticing me and enters the lot to the right of the Babaland. A few minutes later he comes walking around the corner of the building, his hands deep in the pockets of his parka, his denim-covered spider legs moving ahead of the rest of him. He is almost past me and to the Babaland door when he finally notices me. He stops walking all at once. "Aren't you going in?" he snaps, his overlapping teeth chattering.

I smile. "I'm waiting for someone," I say. In all fairness to the poets who will be performing, I don't say who it is I'm waiting for. The rumor that Robert DeNiro is in the audience would certainly cause a stir and distract the audience from the show.

Frank and his lovely wife drive by in their Lincoln. They park and then appear on the sidewalk beside me, Brenda leaning on her husband's arm. "Aren't you going in?" they ask in unison. "I'm waiting for a friend," I say. Brenda's gaze travels down the length of my body. "You look adorable," she squeals as Frank leads her to the door.

Susie comes flying down the street in her red Mustang. She catches the light on the corner and jerks to a halt. Her passenger side window descends. "Did that creep go in without me?" she yells.

"Yup," I yell back.

The light changes and she pulls into the lot. A moment later she comes running around the corner, her narrow heels clicking on the pavement. "Figures," she says as she hurries past me.

Finally, the limo appears. It pulls up to the curve and out steps Robert DeNiro. He looks more tired than I remember from our interview. And I can tell by the way he's looking at me that I've changed some since the interview too. He looks me over approvingly, the way Brenda did. "I'm sorry I'm late," he says, and he smiles the way people do when they know their apology is really unnecessary. I smile back. He stands beside me. We watch the limo disappear. "You cold?" he asks. I shake my head. "You mind if I keep you out here a moment longer? I want to have a cigarette before we go in." "Not at all," I tell him. "In fact," I say, "I'll have one too, if you don't mind," and this in spite of the fact that it's been years since I quit.

We stand in silence, puffing, looking out at the traffic, smiling vaguely. Then he says, "You hear the one about the man who tried to grow spaghetti in his back yard?"

I choke on my smoke. "You got that one from me!" I exclaim. (I backtrack to imagine that I included it in one of my "notes" from the week before.)

He swats his forehead with his palm. He stretches his neck back, exhales smoke, laughs. He shifts his weight from one foot to the other. I rock back and forth too, keeping warm, happy to be where I am, with who I am with, doing what I'm doing... "Well, then how about this one?" he says, and he starts to tell me one I haven't heard, my left arm and his right pressed together against the cold, the two of us falling into a two-step, forward, back, forward, back, keeping warm, keeping close.

And so there we are, me and Robert DeNiro out in front of the Babaland, smoking cigarettes and telling jokes and having ourselves such a good time that I forget all about the fact that there's a show that's going to start in a few minutes, that my paintings are hanging in the lobby. In fact, I am so caught up in the moment that at first I don't even realize that the vehicle stopped at the light is familiar to me. It is Trick, I imagine I realize all at once, on time after all. He has his head at an angle. He is looking right at us, not with surprise but with sadness, a Woody Allen kind of expression. It is almost dark now. There is no sign of recognition on his face. His eyes are bad; he won't know it's me until he parks the car and comes around the corner. All he sees at the moment is a smartly dressed woman and a smartly dressed man, a couple moving to a rhythm that is somehow familiar to him, that makes him remember something he used to have, something he lost, something, he realizes now, that he longs for.

He pulls away, into the lot, then comes walking around the corner. He still stares at us, his expression even gloomier than a moment before. Bobby, who is used to being stared at, doesn't even notice him. But all at once Trick recognizes Bobby. He is about to smile when he recognizes me too. He slows, then stops. His mouth drops open; he turns toward the traffic to conceal it from me. Then he turns back, continues walking, stiff now, his head bent. Just as he is about to pass us, Bobby turns his head aside to exhale a final cloud of cigarette smoke. He doesn't see me extend my hand, brush Trick's arm as he passes. Trick's eyes are narrowed when he glances up at me. He is hurt; he expects to see me gloating. But I'm not gloating. I'm not smiling. I'm just trying to get a message across.

The Babaland door opens, then closes behind me. "Ready?" Bobby asks. "In a minute," I say, and I take a drag from my cigarette. I am lingering on purpose. I want to give Trick a moment to see the way my paintings look hanging on the lobby walls. I take a final drag, then toss the butt into the street. Then I take Bobby's arm and we turn and go in.

A moment of reckoning, I have imagined. I am more than pleased with myself. I unlock the bedroom door so that Trick will be able to get in later. Then I remove both my leather bag and my leather jacket and place them on the floor beside the bed. I sit down and push my feet out of my boots. My nightgown is still over the lamp, but instead of putting it on, I simply toss it onto a chair.

Except for my boots and jacket, I am still fully dressed. I pull down the bedspread, the blanket, and the top sheet and climb into bed that way. I know I will be able to sleep.